Bob Moats

I0567376

TALK SHOW MURDERS

Talk Show Murders

ISBN – 978-0-9903138-2-3

For information and address:
Magic 1 Productions
P.O. Box 524, Fraser MI 48026-0524
Website: http://murdernovels.com
Cover by Bob Moats

Bob Moats

Other Jim Richards series books by Bob Moats

For a preview or to purchase a book, go to
http://murdernovels.com

What a few people are saying about Murder Novels by Bob Moats

"I went online this morning and read your book. I thought at first that I would only read a few pages, but got sucked into it and read all 11 chapters. You are a very good writer! I read quite a bit and often pick up "Airport" paperback mysteries to read on a plane. Most of them are dreadful, with obvious plots. Classmate Murders is a much better story than most."
Ray Zink, Entrepreneur, Minn.

"I got up to chapter ten of the Classmate Murders and decided then to buy the next two books." ... "Just finished your third book, the Dominatrix Murders. I thought it was the best one of the three, didn't want to put it down till I finished it. I looked forward to see how Penny would greet (Jim) every day after her show. Keep the books coming can't wait for the next one."
A. Norris, former Naval Corpsman

"Classmate Murders is well written and keeps the reader involved and wondering what will happen next throughout the book. Showgirl Murders keeps the reader involved throughout the story and keeps you guessing as to who the murderer is until very near the end."
G. Shurig, Kalamazoo

"If you like mysteries and action then don't miss reading this book..."
Jan Schneider, avid mystery/crime reader

"I haven't finished the book yet, when I enjoy a book, I take my time, but I want to buy the other two books. I compare your writing to a Mickey Spillane novel, and I like your style, very narrative. I'm amazed you don't have a publisher yet."
Michael Rasah, Professor of History

"Thanks for making me immortal, love the stories, your friend, Buck."
The real "Buck", George Carver

Extra special thanks to:

Special thanks to Val Brooks who edited this book and for her great suggestions.

Thank you to all the people who purchased this book. I hope you enjoy it as much as I enjoyed writing it for my faithful readers.

The Jim Richards Family of Readers is listed in the back of the book.

Talk Show Murders
by Bob Moats

Chapter 1

Andre Parker was a home decorator, he would go into people's homes to give them a make-over and charge them exorbitant fees. Andre was tied to a chair at the moment and his mouth was obstructed with duct tape. He watched in terror as the man walked around Andre leering and waving the machete. He came close to Andre's face and spit at him, then raised the recently sharpened machete and did a beautiful arching swing at Andre's neck severing his head from his body. The man picked up the head and said "Alas, poor Andre we knew you well".

Earlier that morning, Penny was getting her daily sheets together to study the information for her guest on today's show. The guest was a well known home decorator named Andre Parker. He was big in the Midwest where he traveled to many states to renovate rich people's homes. Penny was happy that they had landed Andre for her show; she was hoping maybe Andre would take a look at her home. She also knew her husband, Jim, would probably razz her about having the flamboyant decorator flitting around her house putting down

6

all her years of decorating the way she liked it. Maybe not a good idea.

Gordy, her producer, finally came in and asked if she had gotten over her sea legs from the ocean cruise that she and Jim had returned from the week before. Gordy had been out of town for the last week and Penny told him that the cruise was very relaxing other than the three murders that they had to endure. Jim caught the killer and everyone was happy, except the victims. She told him more about the cruise and the convention and how everyone worshiped her husband for being the greatest detective in the world. Then she let out a long and loud laugh.

She went serious and said, "Gordy, I need to talk to you some time soon, about the show and my future." Penny spoke while her groupies, as she often humorously called them, started to work on her make-up and hair, making her beautiful for the cameras.

"Penny, is this about you moving to Las Vegas again?" Gordy stood just out of the way of the women waving brushes and lipsticks around.

"Gordy, it's going to happen one day so we may as well deal with it now, are you going to help with a possible change of venues?"

"Penny dear heart, I know some people in Vegas at KLAS that would gladly sell an anchorman and a weather man to have your show. Do you think the networks would go for the change of scene? I mean your Midwestern homespun charm is what carries you everyday."

"Boy do I have them fooled." Penny laughed. "I would have more celebrities to pick from out there, you know that and damn my Midwestern sensibilities, I want to be a glamorous talk show host not Betty Bumpkin dealing with practitioners of home remedies."

Gordy slipped in between the flurry of hands and arms still beautifying Penny to give her a kiss on the forehead. Celeste, head of make-up, whacked Gordy on the back and told him to get out. She proceeded to fix the smear in Penny's make up cause by Gordy's kiss.

At the door, Gordy turned and said, "We'll talk about this, but not now." Celeste shot him a dirty look and he ran out as she threw a powder puff at him.

Celeste asked Penny if she really had thoughts of moving to Vegas. Penny just relaxed in the make-up chair and smiled. "I've been out there twice now with Jim and fell in love with it. We've talked about it but we just haven't gotten to the point of packing it in. Mostly because of my job. Jim's investigating business could easily move and relocate, but my job takes a lot of dealing and set-up to start over somewhere else.

"Well, we would all miss you something terrible if you went." Mary, the hair stylist, spoke now after listening to the conversation.

"Hey, I would take all of you with me if I went, I can't lose a great crew like you guys, you know how to make me look good for the camera."

They all laughed as Steve, the floor manager, called in to say they were ready for taping. The groupies checked Penny one more time and let her up from the chair. Penny gave each one of the women a hug and said she would always be with them no matter where she was. She left her dressing room and weaved her way through the studio to her set and over to the stage. She thought about how she had hosted her show for the last five years since she started her small cable talk show that went to national television after her and Jim's first trip to Vegas for the big television convention.

Steve came up and said that Andre had arrived and would be out shortly after he had make-up applied. Penny laughed knowing that Andre already wore a ton of make-up that marked him as a flamboyant figure in home décor.

A few minutes later, Andre made his grand entrance. He had a voice that penetrated stone and a laugh that bordered on being annoying to dogs. He approached the stage where Penny waited and then they did the one inch spaced fake kiss on each cheek that celebrities did to avoid actual contact.

Andre was seated and his lapel microphone was tested and adjusted low so his voice wouldn't destroy the sensitive device. The show started and Penny stood off by the counter where she always introduced her show from and talked a bit about things that she had on her mind.

She announced her guest and spoke a bit about his credentials and then walked over to the chairs where Andre was lounging. They spoke for about a half hour about his travels and about the places he had transformed for people. They showed numerous photos that Andre talked about in his trademark voice trying to joke about his accomplishments. Penny took questions from her audience that had earlier sat quietly while Andre droned on. The hour long show ended and she thanked Andre for coming out and the end credits ran on the monitor, as Steve yelled that was a wrap.

Penny thanked Andre for coming and they exchanged fake kisses again and he went off with Steve. Penny went back to her dressing room and found me sitting in a chair telling her groupies about the ship board murders. Penny stood at the door listening to me, the senior citizen sleuth, as the media was calling me. I turned my head to the door and smiled when I saw my lovely wife.

"I was just treating your gang to a few pleasantries about our cruise." I said with a sly smile. "I'm sure they are interested in hearing about the murders."

"Not everyone enjoys hearing about murders, Sweetie." She came and gave me a kiss as the women all expressed their desire to hear more about the grisly facts. Penny just shook her head and went to the make-up chair to have her face removed. Celeste was rubbing cold cream over Penny's face as she listened to me relate our adventures. I gave the Reader's Digest version and finished as Celeste was putting Penny's street make-up back on. I always marveled at how fast they were with a liner stick and face brush.

Penny was ready for the afternoon and we said good-bye to the ladies and took our leave. I drove Penny to Roma Paisano, our favorite Italian restaurant. The valet came out and took my restored '89 Crown Vic to the reserved parking and we went in. Nicky Petros, the owner, saw us and came quickly to seat us.

"Miss Penny, you look beautiful as always." He smiled as he pulled out her chair. "James, you look... well, you look no different, but no worse."

"Nicky, you have a great way of making people feel welcome to your establishment." He smiled and called a waiter over to take our orders. I ordered

Talk Show Murders

Veal Parmesan with a bottle of Miller. Penny had Scampi and a glass of wine.

She looked at the glass of beer as I poured from the bottle that was brought quickly and said, "A little early in the day to indulge?"

"I'm still on ocean time. I need to adjust." I said with a sly grin. "One won't hurt."

"How's Buck doing out in Vegas?" Penny asked.

"I talked to him earlier today, he's coming back later this week. He's bringing Maria back to play in the snow like they were supposed to do before we went on the cruise."

We enjoyed our meal and made small talk about her day, as Nicky came by often to make sure everything was perfect. We went to leave and I gave the waiter a generous tip and we said our good-byes to Nicky and drove home.

After Andre had left the studio he hopped into his classic '69 Ford Mustang and drove to his home in Sterling Heights. He pulled in the drive and into the garage, using the remote to open the garage door. He went into the house and over to shut off his home security alarm but found the thing torn from the wall and wires were cut. He panicked and started to turn just as a bag was put over his head and he was pushed to the ground. The attacker was strong; he couldn't get his breath as the person pulled his arms behind him and tied them together. He was then pulled up and made to sit in a chair in what he presumed to be his kitchen. He sat listening but heard nothing, then he heard a grinding noise, and realized it was his fancy professional kitchen knife sharpener. He wet his pants, just as the bag was pulled from his head, before him all he saw at first was the machete.

**

Chapter 2

I pulled into our drive and let Penny out by the porch before I parked, it was the polite thing to do. I parked the car and covered it with the fitted canvas cover to keep the snow from building up on it during the night. We returned from our beautiful Pacific Ocean cruise and came back to snow; unfortunately it didn't go away while we were gone. I hated the cold and mostly snow, even if it had let up a bit and was only a light covering of the crap, but it was still freezing cold.

I went in and found Penny feeding Willy, he wasn't happy to have been left alone but we made up for it with food. I came up behind Penny and wrapped my arms around her as she turned to face me now. I kissed her on the lips and then the nose, I was going for her eyes but she had a stare over my shoulder and let out a quick low scream. I had my Glock out and pointed in the direction of her stare, behind me. I saw the face at the window, it was scary. I had the gun pointed and the figure saw it and ducked to the side. After the mystery man had moved I realized that it was Trapper.

I went to the back door followed by Penny and looked out; Trapper and Becker were sitting on our picnic table laughing. They both looked like they stepped off the cover of Modern Fisherman all decked out in fishing gear, hats with hooks and feathered flies, and vests with stringers and bobbers attached. I had to laugh. Penny went around me and to Trapper; she whacked him on the arm and said, "That was mean scaring me like that."

Trapper smiled and said, "I had no intentions of scaring you, I was just seeing if you two were finally home. I saw Bumbles the clown here with his gun out and got out of the line of fire before he blew a hole in your window."

I went to Becker and held my hand out and said, "Congratulations Barry on making detectives. I had hoped Will would bring you over sooner so we could celebrate but he said you had a big case to take care of?"

Becker smiled and said, "It was a robbery at Harrison Elementary School, not the hard core case I would have wanted, but we caught the culprits, teenagers caught on video. I'm sure it's up on YouTube now."

"Why didn't robbery handle it?" I asked.

"They were short handed this week and being the low man on the totem pole I got roped into it." He made a face.

"Okay, but why are you two out here in those get-ups, fishing is not what I'd expect from either if you." Penny asked.

"We're actually casing a home just up the shore from here. We're watching a husband who may have attempted murder of his wife and he's at the home of his mistress now. So we are watching him and getting some good pictures."

Penny smiled and said, "That's probably Ginger Holmes. She's the neighborhood slut. I hear she has a new man at least once a month. Your guy must be the flavor of the month."

"So you were peeping into the windows hoping to get salacious photos of the criminal?" I said.

"Well Ginger has very big windows and no curtains, so it was easy." Trapper said with a sly smile.

Talk Show Murders

In all the excitement I had forgotten that it was cold and snowy out. "Are you two nuts, it's freezing out here and you're fishing?"

"Ice fishing is legal around these parts; beside our shanty has a good heater." Trapper said. I looked out to the water down the shore and saw the small fishing hut they must have come from. There were a few more spread out but theirs was closer to the shoreline.

"Well, let's get inside before we freeze, or are you going to be deserting your post?" I said.

"Nope we're done, got plenty of good shots of our culprit, and a cup of hot coffee would be nice right now." Trapper grinned. We went in and Penny put on the coffee maker. I didn't drink the stuff and Penny might have a cup or two in the morning, otherwise she didn't really care for it much. The coffee maker was mostly for guests.

We all sat in the family room, Trapper and Becker with their coffee, Penny and I with our beer. Willy finally came out from feeding himself and looked surprised by our guests, he came to me and I picked him up. "I'm sorry we don't have any donuts officers. We may have some cookies though." I said as Trapper gave me a quick finger.

"Well, we're going to have to throw Barry a big party now, just to celebrate his promotion and a good reason to get wasted." I said.

16

"You don't need a party for you to get you wasted." Penny said with a smile.

I ignored her comment and asked Trapper how was LA after we left him and Earl out there after we came back from the cruise. He laughed and said, "We went to see a couple of his old CIA buddies at the LA branch and we had a good time, that's all I'll admit to."

"Hookers and alcohol I'm sure." Penny spoke.

"Well, those were part of it. Did you give that extra flashdrive to your publisher yet?" Trapper asked figuring it's what I would do with all the information that would take down a good number of politicians and mobsters. I had made a copy of the flash drive that contained Valeria Brookson's tell-all book that had come into my possession on our ocean fun cruise and murders. The FBI had the laptop and the original flashdrive, but the book was still Valeria's property even in death.

"I may have slipped it to my agent to peruse the contents. Maybe they will do something with it, maybe not. The royalties go to Lydia Kanaro in Sweden, Val's assistant and lover. I'm sure you remember her, you and Earl were tripping over each other to be with her. We did have a good time on the cruise didn't we?" I laughed and Trapper agreed.

Talk Show Murders

Trapper's cell phone rang and he held up his finger to his lips for silence and answered. He listened for a bit then hung up. "Well, Barry, you may have a chance for a real murder now." He said then looked to Penny. "And it may be connected to you Penny."

Trapper and Becker went to close up the fishing shanty and get their car and said they'd meet us at the precinct. Penny was quiet as we drove over, she held tightly to Willy in his purse. Trapper explained that they got a tip from an anonymous caller than there was a bomb in a box outside the Clinton Township police station. They had the bomb squad come in and after working their magic on the box to see if it was dangerous, they found it contained a human head. With a note. Trapper didn't say what was in the note just that it mentioned Penny by name and we were all being called in.

We pulled into the parking and went in to find Trapper and Becker getting out of their gear and talking to another officer. We held back till they were done and then Trapper's Captain, Josh Barrow, came out of his office and called us in.

We went into the office, Barrows pointed to the seats and sat himself. Barrows was a big African-American and he made Captain early in his career, he was tough. Trapper wasn't fond of Barrows, but respected the man. Barrows eyed Willy but didn't say anything about him.

18

"Here's the poop, the head in the box was identified by the note as being one Andre Parker," he said as Penny made a quiet gasp, having just talked to him this morning. "The note said it was in protest to poor programming by Miss Wicken's show." Penny corrected him saying Mrs. Wickens-Richards. He continued, "what ever, the note identified you by name and said there had better be an improvement in the quality of guests or more deaths would occur."

"What the hell does that mean?" Penny burst out. "How do we determine quality guests and by who's standards!?" She growled.

Captain Barrows sucked on his cheeks for a moment making puckering noises, he did that when he was thinking, and then said, "The note had suggestions, you can read them later. Andre was murdered in his home in Sterling Heights, but the head was dumped here, so Sterling Heights dropped the ball in our court. Not that I want it. Trapper, you and your new boy are assigned to it, and if a certain private investigator happens to keep an eye on the case and his wife, I won't object. Now get out of my office and go find this nut job."

We all went out and over to Trapper's office. We sat and Penny was looking pale, Becker got her a cup of water and offered it to her. She thanked him and asked Trapper what the note said. Trapper opened the file folder he was given by the officer he was talking to when we came in and read, "Warning, this is just the start, I'm going to murder each stupid guest that appears on the Penny Wickens show unless changes are made. I want to see better quality people speaking on topics of importance, global warming, oil spills, health reform, abortion and whatever it takes to enlighten the idiots who watch this mindless drivel that is going on now. Take heed, you have been warned." Trapper put the copy of the note down and looked to us.

"Well, I have been saying to Gordy we should get into more social commentary from our guests, but I'm not going to be dictate by this asshole." she said sadly. "I'm not happy, Jim, can we move to Vegas now?"

**

Chapter 3

It was Friday night and Penny wouldn't have to go back to the studio till Monday. She would be depressed the rest of the night knowing someone she respected had been brutally murdered and it was because of her show.

"It's not your fault that some psycho took offense to your guests, nothing you could do. Does Martha Stewart worry about her guests dying?" I asked as we drove back to our home. "I don't have any cases right now, so I'll come to the studio with you and just nose around, okay?"

Penny gave a half-hearted smile and said that would be nice. I pulled in the drive and saw a car in front of the house, it was Earl Daws. I let Penny and Willy out then Earl came up to her and they went to the door. I parked and went in to find the two of them in the kitchen, Penny was making coffee again.

"So, what brings you to our humble home?" I asked. He took the cup Penny offered and said he needed to talk to me, in private. "No offense Penny, but I have some business to talk about with your husband."

Penny waved her hand and said, "No problem, I'm going to take a dozen aspirins and go take a nap." She kissed Earl on the cheek, picked up Willy and went out. I was hurt that I didn't get a kiss but held my tongue.

"Trouble in paradise?" Earl asked.

"No, I'll explain it to you later, there was a murder and it was in regards to Penny's show. So come on into my home office I set up for just these occasions." I took him to the porch where my desk sat in the corner. I used it to write my stories at home, when the mood struck me. I pulled over a chair and had Earl sit.

Talk Show Murders

"So, what's on your mind?" I asked.

Earl took a sip of coffee and made a face, I said Penny wasn't the best for making coffee and he laughed. He paused and then spoke.

"Well, after Trapper and I got back from LA, I went back to the precinct and before I got to my desk I was called into the Chief's office. He sat looking like the fat ass he is and told me to sit. I did. He then started to tell me our case closings on homicide were appalling and we weren't getting more criminals caught. I told him most of our cases were cold and we had no further leads. He gave me his smug ass smile and said that wouldn't do. He told me I had to close all my cases before the holidays or else I could be reassigned to robbery."

Earl took another sip and made the face again. I asked if he would like a beer, he beamed at that and I went to get us a couple cold ones. I came back and handed it to him, then he continued, "Then the asshole says to me, this doesn't work for him, it makes him look bad. I was getting pissed about then and said that his off the rack suit made him look bad."

Earl smiled at the thought of it, I laughed. "He got all hot and said I better change my attitude or be suspended. I stood, took my badge and gun, plopped them on his desk and said, no I'm changing my job thank you, and walked out. He was bellowing something about getting back there, but I kept going. I grabbed a box from storage and cleaned out my desk. He never came around to bother me. I went to HR and filled out the forms for retirement and walked out on being a cop." He sat smiling.

"So what are you going to do now?"

"Well that all happened last week and I went right over to county and I managed to slip in the licensing paperwork and I am now a licensed P.I., how about that?"

"Must be nice to be an ex-cop to get the paperwork shot through the paper mill. I had to go to school for months to get my license."

"Well you were a rookie, but I have to say since I've known you, you have seasoned well. I've been honored to work with you, so shall we go into business together, like we talked about before?"

His question took me by surprise. I should have seen it coming but he did it so quick, I wasn't ready. "You know many times I thought about hooking up with you and even Trapper. I guess we could give it a go and see if we don't shoot each other." I smiled and held out my hand, he took it and we shook on it.

"Of course, you'll have to get your own business cards and I'm not changing the name of the firm, I like Richards Investigations."

"I don't care what you do, just find me some easy cases to follow and I'll be happy. After everything I have gone through in my law enforcement career, I need some slow time without the heavy thinking. Got a good spousal peeping job for me?"

I laughed and said, "I don't right now, but we could go to my office in the morning and get you set up with a desk and maybe something will come through the door."

"That would be fine, just to sit back and wait for crime to come to me for once. Now what is this thing with my girlfriend?" He smiled widely and downed the beer. I offered him another which he gladly accepted and then I told him what happened at the studio and after.

He sat shaking his head, "As long as Penny wasn't directly threatened, sounds like he wants to punish Penny but not kill her, or he would have made an attempt."

"See you're sounding like a P.I. already." I said. He laughed out loud just as Penny came into the porch and over to plop on my lap.

"Are you two plotting crimes?" she asked. I told her about Earl quitting his cop job and that we were now partners.

"Wow, Mutt and Jeff, comic crime fighting characters. Did Jim tell you about my problem?" She asked Earl.

"Yes he did, I'm sure your life isn't in danger yet, but we'll need to see where this leads before it can become dangerous."

"So you and chuckles here really going to team up? Become the A-minus team?"

"Depends on what his office looks like. I expect luxury in my surroundings, much better than the squad room I had to suffer with."

"Well, we'll have to do a little redecorating before you'll be happy." I realized what I had said about decorating, since the incident with Andre, but the comment luckily went by Penny.

Penny stood and said, "Let's go into the family room to get more comfortable." I asked what was wrong with my lap. She gave me an evil little smile and said, "It was getting a little lumpy if you get my drift." Then she went out. I grinned at Earl and we followed.

We sat and relaxed and talked about Tahiti then Earl related a few of the fun things he and

Trapper got into in LA before coming back to Michigan.

Around 11, Earl said he had to go, he'd see me in the morning and we could go get him settled into the office.

I said, "Trapper is going to have a field day with this news. If he quits too, we can make him the receptionist and he can take calls all day."

"I like that. But Trapper is more of the peeping type; he will be good for surveillance of cheating spouses."

Penny laughed and said she was going to tell Will what we said. I kissed her and said it wasn't anything we wouldn't say to his face. I reached out to shake Earl's hand and said it was going to be good working with him. He smiled, said good-bye and left.

Penny went into the kitchen and came out with two cold ones and handed me one. I popped the top and took a sip. She had already gone back to the couch with Willy jumping up on her lap and we sat quietly for a bit then she said, "I like the idea of Earl working with you, he'll keep you from getting killed."

I tried to ignore her and turned on the television. The news was on and there was the face of Andre Parker starting at us. I heard Penny take a sharp breath and I asked if she wanted me to turn it off, she said no, turn it up. I did.

"Earlier today the decapitated head of the renowned home decorator, Andre Parker was found in a box outside of Clinton Township Police headquarters on Groesbeck Highway, after a false bomb threat was made. Instead of a bomb, the box contained the head of Mr. Parker and a note that we managed to obtain. Mr. Parker had appeared as a guest on the Penny Wickens show earlier this morning and the note stated that if the Penny Wickens' show didn't change their programming to more social conscience topics, more killings of guest would continue. No comment from Miss Wickens or her station has been issued. We will be following up on this breaking news as it progresses."

I shut the TV off and looked to Penny, she was pale again and I said, "Son of a bitching news. Don't take it to heart."

"I have to, these are my people, and I'm not going to let the bastard screw with them."

**

Chapter 4

For the first time since Penny and I shared a bed, she didn't sleep well. I'm not good at sleeping anyway so I stayed up with her most the night. She finally drifted off around 3 A.M. and I followed shortly after. I woke around 6 A.M. and found Penny already up and dressed.

"Where are you off to this morning?" I asked as she flitted around the kitchen getting cereal for herself. I don't eat breakfast generally, but I felt a bit hungry so I grabbed a fruit bar Penny had in the cookie jar.

"I'm going into your office with you. I'm going to play receptionist while you get Earl situated." She replied happily. I guess the little sleep she had was good for her.

"That sounds nice, considering you've only been in my office about three times since I've had it."

"Well, your office is depressing, too sterile, not enough pictures on the walls. Or posters of women in bikinis."

I just stared at her and wondered if she was losing it. "Why would I put posters of bikini babes on the walls of my office?" I asked carefully.

"To cheer the place up or you could put up posters of hunky men, then I would visit more often." She looked to me with her devilish smile and I knew she was yanking my chain. I went to her and slapped her butt and said to behave. She went to the snack bar and ate her cereal, as I went to get dressed. About ten minutes later the phone rang and Penny answered it after checking the caller ID.

"Hello, Gordy. Yes I was at the police station yesterday about it... yes, they showed me the note and I don't like being pushed around... yes I'm concerned about my guests... Who's on Monday?" She was quiet as she listened then had a disturbed look, I came over to her. "Oh, crap, I don't suppose Aunt Jennie could talk about nuclear proliferation? No, I understand, but she's such a sweet woman, I don't want her on the show if it means her life is in jeopardy. Yes, find someone else, someone who will bore the hell out of me and my viewers but won't die because if it. Get some politician to talk about baking a cake, then see what happens. Yes, I'll be in early to have a meeting. Okay, talk later. Oh and Gordy, I'm still moving to Vegas." She hung up and looked to me.

"Aunt Jennie Billson was scheduled to appear talking about her line of cake mixes made here in Michigan, but Gordy is nervous about having her on. She may be a shrewd business woman but I'd hate to be responsible for her demise. This is crap! I really hate being told what to do for my guests."

Talk Show Murders

I gave her a kiss on the cheek and said, "You have another day to mull it over, let's go have a bit of fun with Earl now and get our minds off it." She agreed, put Willy in his purse and we got ready to go.

I pulled into the parking lot of my modest office building and we went in to find Earl sitting in one of the lobby chairs by my office, he turned his head and grinned. "Good morning, fellow detectives." He called out pleasantly.

"How long have you been here?"

"About an hour, the building owner was in cleaning up a vacant office and we had a nice talk. It's upstairs and it's big, two office rooms and a reception area, perfect for an investigation firm." He gave Penny a wink and I said he was trying to run things already.

"Well, from the looks of the size of your office from out here, I'd say we'd need something more sizable."

I unlocked the door and we went in. "Well this is a nice closet, where's the offices?" Earl commented. I stood looking at the one room and a separate bathroom and felt inadequate. "It has suited my needs since I started here, but it is a bit small as I now see it."

"The owner offered us a good rental fee; it's about one third more of what you're paying now." He smiled.

"Boy, you are just into everything aren't you?" I laughed. "Did he say if they furnish it too?"

"Well we did discuss that, the place still has desks and file cabinet from the last renters, we'd have it all thrown in he said."

"Do you know what the office was from the last renters? A call girl service. They had hookers floating in and out of here all day."

Penny gave me a look and said, "You never mentioned that to me?"

"Well I didn't know they were until Trapper turned them in and they got closed down." I defended.

"Damn Trapper, he never could keep quiet about hookers." Earl said.

Penny gave me a poke in the ribs and said, "What else aren't you telling me?"

"Nothing, that's all, no more hookers, can we get off this now and discuss the office arrangements?"

Earl held up some keys and said, "Well, we could go look at the place."

I started out the door glaring at him, "I'm not going to regret taking you on am I? You didn't put down a deposit did you?"

"As a matter of fact..." he didn't finish, he ran ahead and led us up the stairs and into the office, and I had to admit silently that it was nice. There was a small glass enclosed vestibule with the receptionist window and opposite that was a door going into the main waiting room and there were two offices that I could see just off the main room. Each office had a great view of Garfield Road and the surrounding area. Earl gave us the nickel tour and I had to admit it was impressive. There was another smaller room off the side that could be used as another office or for storage and the restroom was huge.

"Okay, did the owner say when we could move in?" I yielded.

Earl pulled out a folded paper and said, "Just sign here and it's ours." He was really like a big kid with his first car. I took the paper and saw the rent wasn't bad for what we were getting; I took out my pen and signed. Earl took the paper and refolded it and said, "Good doing business with you. Shall we move in?"

We spent the rest of the morning moving stuff up to the new office. Earl brought in his box of stuff from his office at the police station and was putting everything in a place. I stood in the hallway thinking about making a sign to say we moved. I went to a box of things I had collected since I had been there and found a good sheet of poster board and a felt pen, then made a moving sign and taped it to the door of my old office. I would miss the place, good memories, but I needed to expand and with Earl it was good.

Earl and I each had private offices now and I yelled to him to stay out of mine. Penny was sitting at the reception desk with Willy on her lap and I remembered that we needed the phone lines moved up here from the old office. I took Earl out to the junction box for the phone service and we did a little hacking by moving the wires around. I called my office number with my cell and Penny picked up, she was surprised it was me. We closed the box and I said, "I'll call the phone company Monday and make it legit and get another line put in for your office, so we aren't fighting over who get to use the phone."

We went back upstairs and into the vestibule and I nearly ran into a man standing looking at Penny behind the open sliding glass window. Penny smiled and said that the man was looking for a private investigator. Earl and I took our first customer into our new office and we had him sit at the round table in the main area we set up for conferences with clients.

"I'm Mitchell McCoy, my wife is missing and I want her found." He spoke quietly.

"Have you been to the police?" I asked.

"No, they said on the phone that they couldn't do anything till she was missing for at least forty-eight hours." He said.

Earl said, "That's standard policy to make sure the missing person isn't just off doing something else, why do you believe your wife is missing and not visiting someone?"

"My wife never goes anywhere without telling me. She's not a brave person; she clings to me until it chokes the life out of me. For her to be gone overnight is just not her."

I looked to Earl and asked him if he wanted to take this since I had to deal with the murder of Penny's guest. He said he'd be happy to and asked McCoy to come into his office and he'd get more information. McCoy stood and asked me, "Is your receptionist Penny Wickens?"

I laughed slightly and said, "Yes she is, she comes in to help us out once in a while." Earl was holding his laugh back and repeated his request to go into the office. They did.

I heard Penny laughing at the desk she sat at, she said to me, "I just started a new career."

**

Chapter 5

Earl and McCoy came out of his office about a half hour later and shook hands. McCoy waved to me as I was taking files out of boxes and putting them in the new file cabinets. He went by Penny and said, "I love your show." Then he went out the door.

"So what do you think?" I asked.

"He murdered his wife and hid the body." He said like it was no big deal.

I stared at him for a moment and then he said, "What?"

"Are you being serious? You really think he whacked his wife?"

"I'm just making an educated guess, his answers weren't very good as I questioned him, he reminded me of another case I had years ago. The husband hacked his wife into little pieces and froze the parts in their upright freezer, then claimed she was missing. Do you know how many claims of missing persons are actually murders by the person filing the report?"

"So then you're going to take the case; you got a retainer I presume?"

He smiled and pulled out a check from his jacket and waved it till I took it and read the thing. It was a fairly good amount, I said, "guilt money maybe?" and I took it to the reception desk and put it in an envelope to deposit.

"We have to talk about how we divide up the fees." He said.

"You get your pay from your cases and I get paid mine from my cases, only fair way. Just don't jump any of my cases. Oh and we split the bills down the middle." I smiled.

"Sounds like a marriage made in heaven. Okay, I have a couple places to check for my new client, just to see if he's handing me a bunch of bull." He put on his overcoat and as he headed to the door, he said to Penny, trying to sound tough, "Hold all my calls, doll." He winked and went out.

"This is fun." Penny said with a chuckle.

"Are you planning on being our permanent receptionist now?"

"Oh hell no, but I'm going to interview them for you, just so you don't hire some buxom blonde bimbo."

"But dear, all P.I. offices have buxom blonde bimbos working for them. Don't you read the pulp fiction books?"

"Well not this one." She stood and put Willy on the floor. "I'm tired and it's getting late, so let's go grab a couple burgers at the drive thru and go home to cuddle. I need loving right now."

"Well then shall we skip the burgers?"

"No, I have better sex on a full stomach." She went into my office to get our coats, as I stood surveying the room. We had brought up the couch I had purchased to take naps on and we put the LCD TV on one wall so we could see it from the couch. It was a good office and I was happy.

We drove through Burger King and then back home. Willy was eyeing the bag of burgers and onion rings and Penny kept telling him to wait. We pulled in the driveway and Penny went inside to give the cheese burger we bought for Willy to him. I came in a couple minutes later after covering the car and we sat at the snack bar eating.

"So what are you going to do about the show critic?" she asked with a mouth full of onion rings.

Talk Show Murders

"Show critic? I guess he could be called that, critics are all killers as far as I'm concerned. I thought about it today, I'll come to the studio and talk to that girl who lines up the guests, what's her name?"

"Joy, she took over for Davey Morgan after he was killed by you during the classmate murders."

"Trapper said to never mention that I did the actual shooting, they claimed Deacon did it, just to protect me."

"Fine; it's Joy who schedules our guests now."

"Okay, I'm going to have a talk with her and see if I can set up a little trap for the Critic. I just need to talk to Trapper and Becker. Do you think Becker would do a good job of talking about his magic show as a guest?"

Penny looked to me and smiled. "You're going to put Barry out as bait for the Critic to attack? That's dangerous."

"Barry wanted to get his feet wet in homicide, this is a good way and Trapper and I will be watching."

"You let Barry get murdered and I'll never forgive you." She said with a bite of burger.

"If he were murdered, I'd never forgive myself, so we'll be protecting him carefully. If Trapper and Becker agree to my plan."

"And if they don't?"

"Well, I thought about putting myself on your show, but if he knows you then he knows me, so that won't work."

"You could use Earl." Penny offered.

"True, we'll see if Becker is up for it first. Are you almost full?"

"Why, getting anxious for sex?" She said with her devilish smile.

I crumpled the burger wrapper, tossed it to the wastebasket and smiled while heading towards the bedroom, "Whenever you're ready, I am."

After a good night's sleep and some good love-making, we started our Sunday morning. "Feel like coming with me to the office to do a bit more arranging?" I asked Penny as she came out of the bathroom looking all refreshed.

"Sure, are you going to hang bikini babe pictures?"

"I do have one that I'll put on the back of my office door." I went to a closet and took out a rolled up poster and opened it. Penny was watching me unroll the thing, and then I turned it to her. She let out a quick little squeal as she saw it was a blow-up of a photo I took of her on the cruise ship in her skimpiest bikini.

"I had this made last week from the picture I took of you and I was going to save it for just the right occasion, I think this is as good a time to put it up." I laughed.

She just stood there looking at the poster and said, "Okay, you can put that up in your office."

We arrived at the building a short time later and found Earl sitting at his desk writing on a pad. Penny let Willy go to run the new place and we went into his office to see what he was up to.

"Good Morning fellow crime fighters." he said as he stood.

"Did you stay here all night or get here early?" Penny asked.

"Got here early, had a talk with the building owner and gave him the paperwork, we are now official."

"I hope you gave him the deposit." I said.

"Nope, he just transferred your deposit from the old office to this one. He was very nice about it."

"So did you find out anything about your client?"

"Well, all the leads he gave me didn't pan out, no one was home. I'm re-grouping and going back out today. Anything on your case?"

"I got a couple of ideas. I called Trapper on the way over and he's meeting us here to see the new place and talk about my plan."

As if on cue, Trapper and Becker blew in the door and stopped in the vestibule looking at us through the glass window. I waved to them and they came in to the main room.

Trapper surveyed the place and said, "Well, crime fighting must be paying better now. Hey, Earl I hear you're out of the club." Trapper smiled as he shook Earl's hand. "Feel good to be away from fighting all the dirty crimes?"

"Yes and not having idiots looking over my shoulder. I do feel good, when you quitting?"

"Not till I get Junior here all broke into my mold. Then I can turn him loose and I can retire happily." Becker smiled at what Trapper just said and Earl gave him congratulations on his promotion.

"So Jim, what sort of devious plan do you have in your mind for catching the killer?"

"Penny gave our perp the handle of the Critic. I like it and if we could all sit I'll explain my idea."

We gathered all the chairs we could and put them around the table in the main room and sat.

"Okay, Barry how good are you about talking on the topic of magic, have you learned enough from me and our late friend Marty to talk for an hour?"

Becker looked at me little blank in the face then a light bulb went on in his noggin. "Ah, you want me to be a guest on Penny's show and hopefully draw out the killer. I can do that." He said it a little too anxiously and Trapper could see it.

"Barry, this isn't like tracking teenagers who robbed a school. We're talking about a crazed killer who decapitated his victim. Do you really feel up to the task?" Trapper was concerned for the young man.

"I guess if you guys are behind me, I'm sure I could do it. I just hope I can talk about my magic for an hour, I've never been on television before."

Penny piped in, "There's nothing to it, you don't see the people at home and the show is recorded so if you screw up we just retake the scene. I think you could do it."

Becker took in her words, thought about it and then flashed a big smile, "Great, let's catch us a critic."

**

Chapter 6

We sat working out the logistics for the plan; I said I'd talk to Joy, the guest scheduler, in the morning. I asked Becker to bring his magic props with him and be prepared to make up his back story in magic. I said I'd work with him on that, although he knew enough about the history of magic, but he was too honest to make up a lie about his life. He had to be someone else, he couldn't be Barry Becker, cop.

Trapper said he'd work with him on his back story later and I said that would work for me. I said, "I'm going to call a magic shop up in Clinton Township and ask them if we could say Barry worked there to have a place for the Critic to find Becker. Then we put him in the store after the show and watch the place. Any suggestions?"

"Do you have a GPS tracker that you can put on Barry, in case you lose him?" Penny asked. I looked to her and smiled.

"Very good idea, babe. Trapper, do you have anything like that we can use?" I asked.

"Yep, I can get him bugged in the morning. Nice call Penny." Trapper said.

"Good, that's all I wanted to say, we set up at the studio tomorrow morning at 6 A.M. if everyone can get out of bed that early." I said.

They all nodded that they would. We finished and I gave Trapper and Becker a quick tour of the place and Trapper asked if the small room off the side was his office?

"I was thinking maybe we could put a desk in the restroom for you." I laughed. We stood around talking for a while then Earl said he had to go do some investigating and he left. Trapper, Becker and I sat working on a story for Becker to tell Penny tomorrow. Penny sat in and made some good suggestions and we finished up. Trapper and Becker left after we agreed to meet tomorrow morning at the studio.

Penny, Willy and I were alone in the office now and I went to put up the poster of Penny on the back of my door so I could admire her great body during the day. She took the car and went out to Kmart's to buy some plants while I organized my desk. She came back with a car load of various fake foliage and potted trees which we brought up from the car. I had to admit the plants made the office look good and being fake, they wouldn't die. I wasn't great when it came to keeping plants alive.

We worked around in the office for a couple more hours then decided to pack it in and go get some rest for the long day tomorrow. We closed up and went to Subway this time to get food then back home.

We were both keyed up about tomorrow so we just had our meal then crawled into bed. Willy jumped up on his favorite chair, did his ritual circle and plopped down to sleep. I had the television on as Penny dozed off and watched it for a while till I dozed off. I woke around 3 A.M. and shut off the TV and rolled over on my side and slept again. The alarm went off at 5 A.M. and I heard Penny groan. We dragged ourselves out and took turns in the bathroom, then dressed. Penny was nervous, which I could understand, she had two days of wondering what was going to happen to her show.

We took separate cars and drove out to her station, past the guard booth as he waved us in and parked. She used her door card to pass through the locked entrance and we went in and over to her dressing room. Gordy was coming down the hallway and saw us. He came up and greeted us then said he wanted to talk, Penny gave me a look, one I could tell was dread. We went into her dressing room and Gordy asked if the groupies could leave for a few minutes. They all went out and Gordy closed the door.

"I got two cops in my office who are here to set up a sting for the killer; I intercepted them in the lobby waiting for you two. I'm a bit leery of using fake guests for the show; it's a matter of the show's integrity even though I understand the purpose for the subterfuge."

"Actually Becker is a magician and is going to be talking about what he knows, so he isn't a fake guest, just a non-social issue kind of guest, one the Critic will not like." Penny said with a touch of huffiness.

"Okay, he's legit, I'm all for it if it catches the killer, but I hope we don't get bit on the ass. The network got wind of the murder and they are concerned and suggested that we pull the show until he is caught."

"Well I hope you backed me up on this, canceling the show only proves he won. I don't like yielding to this asshole."

"The network told us to handle it for now and I hope your little plan works so we can get back to homespun interviews."

Penny scrunched up her nose and agreed. I told Gordy that I felt our scam would work if it all goes the way we planned.

"There will be no danger to the people here since the killer wants to grab the victim and make his statement. So he'd have to wait to get to the victim away from people, we are arranging that. Officer Becker has volunteered to be the bait and we will be watching him closely."

"Okay, the other thing is, we have another guest on today, he is an expert on environmental causes, he'll be talking about recycling. Before you bite my head off, it wasn't my decision, it was the station owners, they want to have this guy talk because they think it will appease the killer. I argued but they were firm. I haven't told them about your plan because I didn't know about it till a half hour ago. So we have to sneak it by them."

Gordy stood, said good luck and went out. I could see Penny was steaming, I just kept quiet.

"Son of a bitch! I'm not happy that they are fucking with my show!" She started to boil, which I've seen her do only one time before this and back then I got as far from her as possible. This time I had to stick by her and calm her down.

"Look we will catch this guy and you can get back to doing what you do best. So relax and let's just get through this day, okay?"

Talk Show Murders

She looked at me, still mad, but I saw a slight yield in her eyes. Her groupies came to the door and asked if it was all right to come in. Penny smiled and said to get to work making her beautiful. I said I was going to gather Trapper and Becker and get things set up.

I went by Gordy's office and found the guys sitting on his couch. "This is no time to relax, let's go!" I led them to Joy's office and found her typing up something on her laptop. "You're not twittering are you?" I asked.

She had a surprised look then said, "No, I'm trying to work out a schedule to appease the gods of TV." She smiled and I introduced her to Barry and Will.

"Joy, please make out a daily sheet for Penny on Barry's background so she has something to go with. But he's not going under his real name and the info will be a bit exaggerated."

I could see her wheels turning and she beamed, "Ah, a sting! To catch the killer, I like it. Okay, Barry let's make out your fake info." She started to type on the desktop computer filling in the form that Penny would use to interview her guest, now known as Larry Decker, magician. She finished the forms and printed them out and called for a runner to take the sheets to Steve, the stage manager.

We thanked her and went to the studio where they taped Penny's show; Steve saw me and came over. I explained the plan to him and he said, "Do you think this will work, the killer won't figure out your guy here is a cop?"

"Well, we're hoping he won't, if Barry, uh, Larry can act the part. I understand you have a snooze guest on?"

"Yep, that's what I hear, talking about recycling paper and cans. Nice and ecological for our murderer."

"Put Barry... Larry on after him. I want the killer to think he has won with Mr. Ecological, then we'll hit him with the fluff piece that should get his attention."

"You got it." He received a call on his headphone from the control room saying they were ready to tape, so Steve excused himself and went to get everyone ready.

I saw Penny come out of the hallway from her dressing room and I had told her to ignore us in case the killer may be in the audience watching the show. We stood off the side as Steve got everyone placed and they coached the audience when to applaud and then Steve called the control room and turned it over to them.

Penny started the show and did her little monologue before introducing her first guest. "I'm sure everyone has seen the news about the unfortunate murder of Andre Parker; this was a despicable act and I am appalled. This is America and a television talk show should be allowed to pick its own guests without being threatened by a terrorist whose agenda is warped. I have to yield to the heads of the station and the networks in regard to who we have as guests now, but I guarantee this bastard killer will be brought to justice soon. I'll get off my soap box now and bring on our first guest, Mr. Kenneth Ripley, from the United States Department of Agriculture who will be speaking on recycling. Please welcome our guest."

**

Chapter 7

Earl sat in front of the tiny home in Shelby Township, watching for curtains to move or some other sign of life. This had been the third time he was at the house and he was getting tired of the wait. The home belonged to his client's missing wife's parents and he wanted to talk to them about his client's relationship to his wife. Earl still had a feeling that McCoy did away with his wife, Margret, and was reporting her missing to cover his tracks. He had seen a number of past cases that were very similar to this one, so the alarm in his head went off early. He had called McCoy when he got up this morning to see if Margret had returned; she hadn't.

There are parts of Shelby Township that are more country than city, homes still spaced out far enough so you couldn't hear your neighbors. This house was in just such a neighborhood and looked to be built in the early 40's as it still had the hard grey asbestos shingles on the sides, the kind that most homes of that time were built with before the EPA banned asbestos from homes. It looked to have only two bedrooms and a tiny living area, as Earl had scouted out the building yesterday and had peeped in the windows and saw that it was a scene from out of his childhood, all frilly and filled with knick-knacks on the walls. Earl's mother loved knick-knacks.

Earl lit up the first cigarette of the week, since he vowed to cut back, then he would finally try to quit them all together. He started smoking around 19 years old, now 32 years past, and had smoked up to two packs a day while he was in the Army. After the Army he joined the CIA as a communications specialist, being in on all the secret dealings going on in private phone conversations from one corrupt politician to another. The persons involved were never accused, just subtly blackmailed by his superiors for favors that the CIA was best known for during the strained relationship with the soviet bloc. His smoking increased caused by the pressure to keep quiet about all the things he knew. It was a strain on him and he lasted about two years before he requested a transfer. He ended up in the elite "Black Ops" team and trained to do things that they didn't write about in the newspapers. Things that caused Earl to smoke even more. He traveled the world on missions that were never spoken in the halls of congress, although the White House was aware of the clandestine activities of their commando raids in parts of the world to gain a foothold for the CIA activities. Earl finally got out of the business and became a law enforcement officer and his smoking waned a bit as he worked up to Lieutenant in Homicide, he slowed up the smoking even more. Now as a private investigator, the pressure was lifted and he decided to quit the habit. Or try at least.

He was reminiscing about his illustrious past in protecting America from itself, when the car pulled into the drive. He tossed his cigarette out the car window and got out. He watched two elderly persons struggling out of their car and cautiously went to them.

"Mr. and Mrs. Bremer? May I have a word with you; it's about your daughter." Earl asked politely.

The couple looked suspiciously to Earl and then the man came around the car towards him, "What's it about and who are you?"

"My name is Earl Daws and I'm a private investigator hired by your son-in-law to find his wife, your daughter. She's been missing since Saturday. Can we talk in private?"

The man just stared for a moment and looked tired, then said, "Come on in. We just got back from the store, if you could help bring in our groceries, that would be real nice."

Earl helped take the paper bags from the trunk of the car as Mr. Bremer said, "Don't abide by plastic bags, bad for the environment."

They all carried their share and went into the house. Earl was right about the quaintness of the interior, like it was stuck in time. He put the groceries on the small counter and then Bremer invited him into the living room. He pointed Earl to a rocker that was covered by a quilt and Earl sat carefully afraid the thing might break under his weight, it look like an antique. Most of the furnishings look to be antique. So did the Bremers.

They looked to be in their late seventies or early eighties, and both had grey hair. Mr. Bremer was a tall gaunt man looking like he lived hard. Mrs. Bremer reminded him of the woman on the box of cookie mix only heavier.

He surveyed the room and saw a number of photographs in quaint frames of the family; Mom, Pop and their baby girl. He didn't see any pictures of Mitch with their daughter, just a lot of the three of them. Strange there were no photos of their wedding or anything else to even suggest that they had a son-in-law. Mrs. Bremer sat on an easy chair and Mr. Bremer sat on the Lazy-Boy recliner, but didn't recline.

"I don't know if you are aware that your daughter has been missing, are you?" He asked.

"Mitchell had called yesterday to ask if she had been here, we told him she hadn't been. He said he was concerned that she was gone so long."

"Have you heard from her in the last two or three days?"

Mrs. Bremer spoke now, "She called me Friday saying she and Mitch had an argument and she was upset, we didn't talk long since he was just getting home, so I said I'd call her later. I never did. I hope she's all right." She took on a very sad face and Earl was not liking Mitch now.

"Well, I'm going to do my best to find her, hopefully she may have just gone off with a friend and she'll return on her own. May I ask a few personal questions?"

The both nodded and Earl continued, "Mrs. Bremer, you said that your daughter and Mitch were arguing, do you know what about?"

"Oh, it's always the same, she didn't like Mitch staying out so late and his drinking, and it was causing problems for the two of them. One time Marge mentioned that they were having financial problems." Mrs. Bremer said and then had another distressed look on her face. Earl could tell it was not a happy marriage for Mitch and Margret.

"Does Margret have any close friends locally that she may have gone to, someone she could trust to keep her safely away?"

"Well, there's Libby, Margret's friend since early on. She lives here in town; I can give you the address if you want?" The woman asked with a smile now, like she had something that may help.

"That would be great, and if you have any other places she may have gone, that would really help." Earl smiled back.

"Oh, goodness, where are my manners, would you like some lemonade, Mr. Daws?" The woman asked.

"Why that would be real nice, Mrs. Bremer." The woman went to the kitchen to get the address book and some lemonade.

Mr. Bremer waited till his wife was out of the room and leaned forward, "I think Mitch is a bastard, I never liked him. Always drinking up a storm and the way he treated my daughter, well I would have told him off but I feared he might hurt her."

Talk Show Murders

"Do you think he may have done something to her?" Earl asked cautiously.

"I do, and I want you to find out and get his ass convicted. I'll pay you good to do that; I have some bonds put away for the future I can cash."

Earl smiled, "That won't be necessary Mr. Bremer, Mitch is already paying me well enough. I'll take him for more if possible." Bremer smiled and said, "You do that sonny, I'd appreciate it."

"I need to ask a delicate question, did your daughter have a life insurance policy on her?"

"I couldn't tell you if she did or not, but I know our family insurance man may help out with that information. I can call him and have him give you what you want to know." He offered.

"That would be fine, Mr. Bremer." Earl spoke as Mrs. Bremer came back in the room with a piece of paper and a tray of glasses filled with lemonade. She handed the glasses to her husband and Earl and sat.

"I wrote down a few friends that I know of who Margret may go to if she had problems, they all live nearby." She said.

"If they live nearby, wouldn't your daughter get in touch with you?" Earl asked.

"I can't speak for Margret, but she may have been embarrassed to call, she knew we didn't approve of Mitch." She answered.

Earl tasted the lemonade and it was good, fresh squeezed from good lemons, complete with pulp and just the right amount of sugar. He really liked it here, and the lemonade was great but he drank it down with haste and apologized for having to leave, but he had to get moving. Earl gave Bremer his new business card that he had ran off on his computer the day before and asked Bremer to call him about the life insurance. Mr. Bremer stood and shook Earl's hand and walked him to the door.

Earl went out to his car and sat in the driver's seat looking at the addresses on the slip of paper. What he didn't see was a car parked down the road, with a man sitting watching Earl through binoculars.

**

Chapter 8

Penny walked over to her guest with trepidation; she had always wanted her show to be light, happy and fun. In the past she had numerous celebrities on, along with strippers who showed how to exercise by pole dancing. She dreaded talking about things like recycling, not that those topics weren't important, but it was not what she wanted for her show; leave that to the "View" or Oprah.

Her guest, Kenneth Ripley politely stood as Penny approached the easy chairs where Penny interviewed her guests. She asked him to sit, he did and Penny sat on the chair next to him but on the edge of the seat, leaning forward. "Mr. Ripley, you are here to talk about recycling, it's that correct?"

"Oh please, call me Ken; yes I will be explaining how people can save the planet by turning waste into useful items." Penny winced at the thought of garbage being useful.

"Well, Ken, go ahead and tell us." She said, with not much enthusiasm from her voice. Ripley went into what sounded like a canned spiel for the USDA and their efforts to clean up the planet one empty can at a time. I could see that Penny's eyes were glazing and once during a commercial when Ripley wasn't looking she held her finger, pointed like a gun, and shot her brains out.

Back from commercial, they talked some more and Ripley showed slides of landfills that had been cleaned up and made into parks. I imagined the smell from the ground as children played.

After a half hour, Penny signaled Steve to get Ripley off and on with our plan, so Penny thanked him for coming and announced that after the station break she would bring on a special guest. They cut away and Steve came to get Ripley and led him off the set. Barry was bouncing; I asked him what he was doing. He said he was nervous and probably needed to pee. I pointed to a rest room off the side just for stage hands and he ran in. Steve came over and I told him where Barry was, he smiled. A few minutes later Barry came out and Steve had a lapel mic attached to him and then took him to the stage. Penny smiled at him and whispered to just relax as Barry sat in the chair.

Steve went back to his podium and called the count down, "Places everybody, in 4... 3... 2..." and pointed to Penny on the silent one. Penny smiled at the camera and said, "Welcome back, I am delighted to introduce our next guest, Larry Decker, who at the age of twenty-four has been into magic for a good number of years. He has been out to the magic convention in Colon, Michigan where we ran our show from for five days last year, and he is here today to talk about, what else, magic. Welcome Larry."

I was just as nervous for Barry as he was for himself; I hit the restroom after he came out. Trapper just stood viciously chewing on a toothpick, I had never seen him do that, but it was something to help with his nerves, I presumed. Barry was holding up to Penny's questions and he did very well on the brief history of magic that he related. Penny had Barry do a couple of close-up tricks and he performed flawlessly, I was proud of him. I had been performing magic for over forty years and yet Barry was a natural in the year I had worked with him, building up his talent ever since we got back from the magic convention. He was doing great and Penny was finishing up his segment by announcing, like we arranged, that Larry worked at Fun Fair Magic Shop on Gratiot just north of Fifteen Mile in Clinton Township and to stop in to talk magic with him. She said good-bye to Barry AKA Larry and then good-bye to her home viewers. The credits ran on the monitor and Becker came over to us with a stupid grin on his face.

Trapper leaned to me and said, "Now he'll be unbearable." Penny was heading to her dressing room and gave me a wink as she passed by. She knew I would be taking Becker to the magic shop and Trapper and I would be watching for the Critic. We thanked Steve and headed out to our cars; Becker, Trapper and I all had our own vehicles and we followed each other closely. Trapper had taken out three walkie-talkies from his precinct, one for each of us to keep in communication. I tested mine and both of them answered the call.

We drove up and over to Gratiot Avenue and up to Fun Fair, Becker parked in the back parking lot followed by Trapper. I parked in front of the next building on the street parking. I could see the front of the magic shop and the front of the alleyway going between the buildings to the back parking lot. Trapper called and said he was situated where he could see the back of the building and the alley as it emptied to the lot. Becker called one last time, carefully in case he was being watched and said he was going inside. He exited his car and walked through the alley to the front entrance of the magic shop building. He caught a quick glance my way to see where I was and then went in. I sat back waiting for a long night ahead.

~~*~~

Earl pulled into the driveway of the address he was given by Mrs. Bremer and walked up to the door of the townhouse, knocking with the fancy brass door knocker. He waited a minute then knocked again. He could hear a female voice yelling to hold his horses and the door flew open. Before him was a leggy redhead in a t-shirt and no pants, the t-shirt went down below her crotch showing just her well-toned legs. She was well built and looked to be in her late forties, but still very attractive and youthful, reminding him of Penny. Earl was a bit taken by her looks and then had to shake himself back to reality.

"Miss Garver?" Earl asked.

The woman looked at Earl and broke out in a big smile, "Yes handsome, I am, and who might you be?"

Talk Show Murders

Earl pulled out his card and handed it to her and said, "Earl Daws, private investigator, may I speak with you?"

She looked at the card, grinned and said, "Wow, good looking and a private dick, I like that." Earl was concerned about the dick remark. It was an old term for a detective, not used much anymore since J. Edgar Hoover passed on.

Earl cleared his throat and said, "Are you a friend of Margret McCoy?"

She gave him a concerned look now and said, "I am, is there something wrong with Margie?"

"She's been missing for the last three days and her mother gave me your address. Have you seen Marge in the last week?"

"Come in please, we'll talk." Earl went into the townhouse and she led him to what he presumed to be her family room. Earl was behind her and was reading the printing on the back of her t-shirt, "I have the vagina, so I make the rules!" Earl grinned. She pointed him to a chair and she sat on a straight back wooden chair across from him. She wasn't being modest about having her legs spread a bit giving Earl a nice view of her pink panties. She wrapped her feet around the legs of the chair causing her panties to be exposed even more. Earl tried to maintain eye contact with her.

She smiled and said, "I'm sorry, am I embarrassing you?" She pulled her feet from the chair legs and then crossed her legs so to close up the view. She grinned.

"Miss Garver, if you have any information about Margret, I'd like to hear it."

"Please call me Paula, and I talked to Margie last Friday, she was really upset. Seems she and the ass she's married to had a big fight and she wanted to get away somewhere from him." Earl perked up hearing that.

"Where might she have gone if she did get away from him?" Earl asked.

"Who exactly are you working for Mr. Daws?"

"I'm not at liberty to say who my client is, let's just say it's a person who's concerned about her."

"If Mitchell is looking for her and she ran away, I wouldn't try too hard to find her Mr. Daws."

"Please call me Earl. Why do you say that?"

"Well, Margie was afraid of Mitchell, he could be such an ass and mean. I've tried to get her to leave Mitchell for a long time now. I hope she has finally left him."

"So, Paula, you think she may have run out on him and she's was not harmed?"

"Oh, I didn't say that, she might have been harmed, I hope not, but it would be a good reason that she is missing. If you know what I mean?"

"No I don't, please tell me."

She leaned towards Earl and said quietly, "He was capable of killing her, and he has threatened her in the past."

Earl took this in to consideration and thanked her for her candor. "You have my card if you hear from her, have her call me." He stood and she slowly got up from the chair.

"May I call you anyways?" She asked with a grin.

"Well, I don't see why not, but I'm pretty busy for the time being."

"Well, I'll call until you aren't busy, if that's good for you?"

"If I don't answer, leave a message." He grinned back and they went to the door, she gave him a kiss on the cheek and said there's more if he liked. Earl smiled and left.

Earl reached his car and looked back, he could see her standing at the window, her T-shirt was now gone and she was just in her pink underwear, with a big smile and threw Earl a kiss.

Earl made a mental note to watch out for her. What Earl didn't see, again, was the man in a car watching out for him.

**

Chapter 9

I felt like I did back when Buck and I worked security at the car dealership. Sit around and wait for something to happen, boring then, boring now. I thought about Buck and wondered how he was doing out in Vegas. I pulled out my cell phone and dialed Maria's number, she came on.

"Jim how are you doing? You survived the cruise yet?" She said after seeing it was me by the caller ID.

"I'm fine, is the big guy there?" I asked.

She laughed and said he was, Buck came on the phone and yelled, "Jimmy, wazz up?"

"Oh I'm sitting out in the snow and cold doing surveillance on Barry Becker." I smiled.

Talk Show Murders

"Becker, what did he do to deserve surveillance?"

"He didn't do anything, but he is part of a little set-up we have going to catch a killer." I said and then explained the whole story to him.

"Wow, Penny must be upset."

"To say the least. We hope the Critic goes after Barry and Trapper is out back of the building watching for him." I was scanning the cars that pulled in and out of the alleyway to and from the parking lot. I tried to keep track of them and wrote down their plate numbers just in case.

"You need help? I was planning on coming back next week but I can cut it short if you need me."

"I can always use you to help, but just enjoy your stay away from the hell hole of cold here, and if I need you I'll call. Oh and I forgot, we have a new office and a partner, Earl Daws." I explained what had gone on with Earl joining and our moving upstairs.

"I like! Earl is good people and it would be easier for me to start our security business like we talked about awhile back with him helping the investigating part."

"Yep, we can still do that, or I should say you can, that's your baby. I have to cut this short, it's almost time for Becker to leave the shop so I'll keep you informed and talk later." I said as we finished. I watched the front for a bit, and then saw Becker coming out. He didn't acknowledge me but I could see he was looking my way. He walked to the alley and turned into it to go to the back parking. I called Trapper and told him Barry was on his way back, he acknowledged. I waited as a car pulled out from the alley, there was one person in the thing, I noted the plate number as I had for all the vehicles coming and going, just as the car pulled out onto Gratiot and headed south on the divided highway. I was watching the car going away when Trapper called and asked where Becker was.

"He went down the alley, he didn't come out?"

"No, I'm pulling over to see up the alley." He clicked off and seconds later, he came back on, "He's not in the alley, where the hell did he go?"

I thought about the only car that pulled out after Becker went into the alley and asked Trapper if a car had left the parking and went into the alley a few minutes ago, he said a car had left, but it was about ten minutes ago.

"Crap! Get up here now, the Critic has Becker!" I started the Crown Vic and pulled over to the front of the magic shop just as Trapper tore up the alley. I jumped out, locked the car and ran to Trapper's unmarked squad car. I yanked open his door and got in, yelling to turn right, down Gratiot. I said to get the GPS device up and running, he flipped on the switch on his dash and the thing lit up with tiny dots showing our location and Becker's as they were moving ahead of us.

"The Critic must have been waiting in the alley for Becker to walk through, then somehow got him into his car and drove right past me, shit! The car was a late model dark brown Chevy sedan, license number RJM-3849." I said as we sped down the road. Trapper got on his police radio and called for assistance. The blips on the screen were almost converging, just as the red blip representing Becker's location turned off the highway ahead. Our green blip got up to the turn off and Trapper ran a stop light to follow. We were coming up on the side street, to the red blip where it had stopped. Trapper was calling our location to the back-up that we hoped would get here quickly and then Trapper had to stop his car.

We were staring at the GPS locator and saw the red blip was still stationary. We looked around but saw no cars on the side street we turned on to. The city doesn't allow street parking during the winter, so all cars were off the road and the only cars we saw were in the drives of the homes along the street. We were almost right on top of the red blip but didn't see the car in question. I looked back to see the flashers of the patrol cars coming down the street and pull up behind Trapper. I looked over to the house next to us and could see a light on in the garage window and told Trapper about it.

Everyone exited their cars and gathered, as Trapper related what had happened. I was watching the garage and saw movement in the light; I said he's on the move. Everyone ran to the garage with guns drawn and came up just as the small entryway door opened and a man stepped out.

"Freeze, hands up now!" Trapper yelled and the man looked startled. The patrol officers grabbed the man and cuffed him, I ran into the garage and found Becker lying on an old couch bound and gagged. I pulled the tape off his mouth but he didn't respond, although he was breathing. Then I saw a small dart stuck in his side and pulled it out. Trapper was standing next to me watching, he kneeled down and was carefully slapping Becker's face. After a few minutes Becker started to come to. I had his wrists and legs cut loose and we sat him up.

He looked at us through glazed eyes and asked where he was. Trapper and I just laughed for happiness that he was all right. The Patrol cops had the man in back of one of the squad cars as we came out of the garage, Becker still a little weak.

We had all gathered back at Clinton Township precinct and had the man in the interrogation room, just sitting looking rather stupid. He just sat looking around the room and making faces at the mirror. Becker had told us that he was walking down the alley past the car when he heard a popping noise and felt a sharp pain in his side, which was all he remembered until we woke him. I said the man was waiting in the alley and hit him with a tranquilizer dart and then must have pulled him in the car.

We watched the man for a bit then Trapper said it was time to go question the guy. Becker and I stayed in the observation room as Trapper entered the other side of the mirror. The man was sitting in a daze and jumped when Trapper burst through the door.

"Mr. Herman Kepler, as your driver's license says you are, you are here for kidnapping an officer of the law and possible murder charges in the death of Andre Parker. How's that sound so far?"

"I never killed no one, yeah, I grabbed the magic guy but just to protect him, that's all. He was a cop too, wow, I didn't know." The man was rolling his eyes as he talked; he looked to be either on drugs or having a mental problem.

"Protect him from whom?" Trapper asked.

"That nut guy who killed the gay decorator. Man, there are all kinds of nuts running around out there." He mumbled.

Trapper look to the mirror and shrugged. He turned back to Kepler and asked, "Please explain your mission to protect the magic guy?"

"Yeah... uh, I saw that the nut killed that gay guy and he said he'd do it to any other crappy guest on that woman's show. I saw the magic guy and said to myself... Herman, that guy is going to die. So I got my tranq gun from a job I had at the Detroit zoo and went to the magic place he worked at. When I knew he was coming out, I waited in the alley and popped him with the dart. I pulled him in the car and went home. I was only trying to protect him." He was whining about it now.

"Where were you last Friday around noon to 3 P.M.?" Trapper asked leaning over because Herman had his head on the table now. He didn't respond so Trapper whacked his hand on the table causing Kepler to jump again. Trapper repeated the question.

"I was in the free clinic down off Chene in Detroit all day for observation; they said I had an episode that I could have harmed other people while I was in a bank on Cadieux Avenue. The cops took me there; I was a bit drunk then." He smiled and put his head back down on the table.

Trapper stood and sighed. He left the room and came back to us saying, "I don't think he has the brains to murder Parker, but after pulling this stunt with Becker, I'll run his alibi and see what it comes up with."

We walked out of the observation room when another detective came up and whispered something to Trapper. He got a pained look on his face and turned to Becker and I, "Seems we were watching the wrong victim, they just found that agriculture guy, Ripley, over in Warren, hanging from a tree in a park."

**

Chapter 10

It was almost eleven in the evening and I was wearing down from the long day and early rise. We had spent the last hour and a half with the Warren police watching them process the body and crime scene of Kenneth Ripley. Trapper was given cooperation by the Warren police since the murder spree started under his jurisdiction. He got a copy of the note left in Ripley's pocket, making new demands and I finally told Trapper and Becker that I was going home to crash for the night. Trapper managed to get me an extra copy of the note so I could examine it and he had one of his patrol officer's drive me to get my car at the magic shop.

I thanked the cop and went to my car, noticing a note under the windshield wiper. I pulled it out and read it under the street light. My blood chilled and not from the cold.

It read, "Richards, clever of you to try and divert me from my quest to improve your lovely wife's show, but it doesn't matter, I am too clever for even you, the great detective. Just watch out or someone you care for may be the next victim."

I pulled out my cell and called Trapper and read it to him. He was not happy.

"I don't like his reference to hurting someone I care about, that could be any number of people but I'm thinking Penny, so I'm going home to check on her and call Buck back to help. I'll talk to you in the morning." I hung up and got the car going toward home, I called her just to make sure she was all right. She came on sounding sleepy and I apologized for waking her. She said she wasn't sleeping, just sitting with Willy waiting for me; I told her I was on my way and hung up. Damn this bastard!

I got to our drive and dreaded having to tell Penny about Ripley, and I would have to mention about the note on the car. I couldn't keep an important piece of information like that from her, she deserved to know and be prepared for the worse. I pulled in and parked, covering the car. I was looking around, if the killer knew where my car was at the magic shop, he would have to know where we lived. I didn't like it one bit.

I came in and went to the couch where Penny was resting, the television was off so she hadn't seen the news yet. She sat up as I came to her and I sat next to her not knowing where to start. She saw something was wrong, took a breath and asked, "Is Barry all right?"

"He's fine but, well you're going to hear about it anyway, Ripley, your guest today, was murdered over in Warren."

Penny took a big breath of air and looked stunned. "Hell, we put him on the show because he was someone the Critic would like, why the hell did he have to kill him?" She was stressing now and I waited till she stopped breathing heavily.

"The note we found on him said he wasn't good enough, the Critic wants more social issues, more political. Hell, I don't know why he just doesn't watch "Face the Nation" or "Meet the Press" if he wants political. Why pick on your show? He said that recycling was good but not what he wanted to see. He wanted more social issues, whatever that means."

I could see tears rolling down Penny's cheeks; I took a tissue from the box on the coffee table and gave it to her. "Did he say anything about Barry?" She asked.

"Well that brings up another touchy subject. The Critic left a note on my car saying he knew what we had tried to pull off today. I don't think he would have tried anything with Barry since the

Critic knew he was a cop and not just a guest." I thought I would wait till tomorrow to tell her about the incident tonight with Barry's kidnapping. "It still doesn't excuse the death of Ripley, but this guy knows things we are doing, and I don't like that." We were quiet for a moment then I said, "He also threatened someone I care about, no names mentioned, just someone. I don't like not knowing, so I'm calling Buck back to watch you while I help Trapper find this scum."

Penny didn't say anything, just nodded. I think she was still a little stunned by all of it and was not feeling much right now. I hoped she wasn't giving up on everything she worked so hard to build up and I told her so. She looked to me, kissed my cheek, was quiet for a moment and said she wasn't giving up on anything; she would be fine in the morning after she had some sleep.

Although she tried, she couldn't sleep, so she took a couple sleeping pills we had for nights I couldn't sleep and she finally drifted off. We were in the guest bedroom, I told her it was to throw off the killer, just in case he came around, and had my Glock on the bed stand next to me.

We awoke around 6 A.M. and were getting dressed when the house phone rang, I looked to the caller ID, it was Penny's studio. I just felt it was going to be bad news. I answered and Gordy asked if Penny was available. Penny was standing in the doorway from the kitchen and she had a look in her eyes that I could tell she knew. She took the phone and said hello.

She was listening and then said, "So they aren't even going to give us a chance to put on the guests he is demanding?" She listened more then said, "Fine, call me when they get their heads out of their asses Gordy." She slammed the phone down and gave me a look that reminded me of when she had stomach cramps from a bad bowl of chili.

"Damn station owners have pulled the show and they want to put a cooking show in its place until the killer is found. The station told the network that they wouldn't be liable for more murders from here on. The networks are saying the ratings for the show are way up after the first killing, the media news has been building the murders up, blood thirsty fools, so now the network is arguing with the station owners over who gets the say as to whether the show is pulled or not. Gordy says the network is going to show reruns for now until they talk to the lawyers about the contracts."

I went to Penny and put my arms around her, she grabbed on to me and buried her head in my shoulder and I could tell she was crying. I didn't know what to say to make her feel better; I was never good at comforting people.

"Why don't you come into the office today and you can play receptionist. I can treat you like a dame and have you take dictation." I said and I could hear her giggle a little. She pushed back and held her head up, wiping the tears with her hand and said, "Can I wear a short skirt and put on the Marilyn Monroe wig I have?"

"Sure, but you'll have to put out for the boss." I smiled to her as she looked into my eyes. She kissed me on the nose and said, "Only if he gives me a raise, I don't put out for nothing."

"Deal, now let's get ready, and feed Willy before we go so he isn't begging us all day." I went to finish getting ready and pulled out my cell phone, dialed Maria's number again and Buck answered this time.

"Jimmy, it's all over the news here about the killings from Penny's show, you want I should come back?" He said sounding concerned, Buck had a good heart.

"I'd really appreciate it if you could, I'll make it up to you."

"Don't even think about it. Besides, Maria is coming back with me to enjoy the snow she missed when we went on the ocean cruise. She and Penny can keep each other company while I watch the both of them. I presume you want me to protect Penny now."

Talk Show Murders

"You are a psychic, my man. Yes, and this morning the station pulled Penny's show until the killer is caught, so he may not like that and decide to go after Penny. That's my guess for now. Penny is a bit miffed about being pulled off the air, I really understand the station's point, they don't want to be liable for putting people up to be slaughtered. But it's going to be hard on Penny. I'd really appreciate you coming back to watch over her."

"No problem, my friend, we'll grab a flight back ASAP and I'll call when I know."

I thanked him and we cut the call. I told Penny that I had called Buck and he and Maria are coming back. She smiled and said, "Good, Maria and I can go shopping to help forget all this crap."

I had to laugh to myself, Penny always thought of shopping when things were going crazy. We gathered our things along with Willy and drove over to the office and up the stairs. We entered the place, the door was unlocked, I figured Earl was in early and then found an attractive red-head sitting at the reception desk.

She smiled and said, "May I help you?"

**

Chapter 11

I looked to Penny and winked. I turned back to the girl and said, "Yes, we need to hire a private detective, do you have one here?"

"Oh, we have the best," she said as she turned her head towards Earl's office and yelled, "Hey, Earl got some people here looking to hire you."

I couldn't see Earl in his office through the vestibule window overlooking the main room. Suddenly I saw Earl's head pop up from behind his desk and gave us a half awake look, then he focused and saw me grinning at him. He jumped up and came staggering out of his office pulling his shirt together and buttoning it up. He looked like he had a rough night.

"Uh, Paula these people belong here, this is Jim Richards and his wife Penny Wickens." Earl said as he opened the vestibule door for us. Penny breezed into the room as I walked past Earl grinning. He closed the door and said, "Guys, this is Paula Garver, a friend of my missing woman."

"Were you interrogating her?" I asked with a big smile.

"Ah, Paula could you go into my office and wait for me?" Earl asked the stunning red-head, she smiled, stood and headed to the office but stopped, turning she said, "I know you, you're that woman from the TV, a talk show right?" Penny just said yes and Paula went off without another word. Earl grinned and said, "She's some woman, we hit it off real fast."

"What you do, is your business." I was really trying to hold back a laugh. Penny smacked the back of Earl's head, gently but firm; he yelped slightly then smiled at her.

"You're a horndog Earl." She laughed and went to sit at the reception desk. She put Willy down and the dog ran straight for Earl's office and stood looking at Paula. I watched Willy wondering what he was doing when she pulled out a donut and broke off a piece and gave it to Willy. He was no dummy.

Earl pulled me away from both the women and said, "I didn't think you'd be in this morning, what with the murder last night I figured you'd go to see Trapper."

"Penny's show was pulled from it's time slot because of the murders so I brought her here until I figure out what to do today. How's your case coming?"

"Yesterday I talked to a whole lot of people who knew my client McCoy and every one of them said basically the same thing; he was a prick and probably did away with his wife. I just need to prove it now."

"How'd you get hooked up with the flaming babe?" I asked.

"She was the first one I talked to and the last one, she is some wild thing and I like red-heads. I think I could get used to her, as a girl friend only, nothing serious. I need my space."

"Yes, and you need to take her to your place, not the Richards Investigations motel."

"Well it wasn't planned, she came here looking for me and what could I do, and she attacked me."

"You mean to tell me, Mr. Black Ops boy was caught with his pants down?"

"Yeah all the way to my ankles." He grinned.

"Well, we'll see how Penny and her get along before you make her a permanent fixture here. Are you thinking of making her the receptionist?"

I looked over and Penny was gone, I walked to Earl's office followed by Earl and found Penny sitting in the client chair next to Earl's desk, Paula was sitting in Earl's chair, they were just laughing. Willy was on Earl's desk sitting up for Paula.

Talk Show Murders

I stepped into the room as Penny turned and said, "This is for women only, you men go play detective or whatever it is that you two do."

I nodded to Earl and he followed me to my office. I sat at my desk, Earl took the client chair. "I hope this isn't going to bite us, if the two of them get to plotting." I reached for the phone on my desk and dialed Trapper. He came on after a few rings and asked if Penny was all right.

"Yeah, her show was pulled and she's not happy but I got her relaxed for now. Do you have a spare officer you can have come to my office to watch her while we play detective? Buck is flying back from Vegas and I want her watched until he gets here."

He said he did and would have him over in a short while. I said, "I'm concerned that the Critic may come after Penny now that he has no guests to kill. After your guy comes by I'll be over and we can work out something. I don't know what, but maybe we can figure something out." He said he'd wait for me then hung up.

"I looked to Earl and asked, "What does the hot tamale do for a living besides doing you?"

"She doesn't do anything, she has a generous alimony check each month from her ex and she lives well. So I thought she could hang around here and watch the office while we are out, she likes the idea."

"Do we have to pay her?"

"That's the beauty of it, she doesn't care to be paid, just to get out of her place and be in the exciting world of criminal investigations. And also to see me, she is one wild woman."

"Yes, you already covered that. Did you did tell her this can be a boring job?"

"Oh, yeah, I gave her the whole talk about the business, she didn't care, there's the couch and the TV, she says she'll be happy."

"Okay as long as Penny has no problem with her, I'm fine with it, besides she is an eye full."

Penny came to the door and said that she wanted Paula for the receptionist. I asked if she wasn't going to interview anyone else, she simply said nope, and went back to Earl's office. "Well I guess that answered that."

Penny and Paula went back to the reception desk and Penny was giving Paula instructions on what to do. Earl and I sat around for about twenty minutes talking about the murder last night and Earl's case when the door opened and in walked Becker and Trapper.

Paula smiled and said "May I help you."

Talk Show Murders

Trapper just looked stunned and then said, "Yeah, I'm here to see Mr. Richards." He started to break into a smile as he saw Penny sitting off to the side. Penny introduced Trapper and Becker to Paula and they came in.

The two of them came to my office as they pulled a couple chairs with them. Suddenly Paula appeared at the door and asked if any of us would like some coffee. Earl and Trapper accepted, Becker and I declined. I reached over to the corner of my office where I had put in a cube refrigerator and pulled out a Pepsi for me and asked Barry if he wanted one, he nodded his head and I got one for him.

Trapper was looking out the door at Paula, she had on a dark, short, tight skirt, spiked high heels, purple silk blouse open at the neck and also opened two buttons precariously lower, allowing a slight view of her black lace bra. Her hair was long, straight and a bright reddish auburn. Most of all she was beautiful and built for power.

I snapped my fingers at Trapper and he shook his head back to me, "Were did you find her and is Penny letting you keep her?"

"She's Earl's squeeze and Penny likes her so we may keep her." I laughed.

Earl snarled at Trapper, "Just keep your hands off, she's not a hooker, she's a real classy woman. The kind you don't like."

Paula came back with a carafe of coffee and two mugs all on a tray that Penny had bought earlier in the week. Penny knew I didn't drink coffee but thought we should have the equipment in case. Paula put the tray on my desk and said to enjoy and went out. I winked at Earl and he grinned.

Trapper put a tan folder on my desk, "This is a copy of the Warren police reports on the killing last night of Ripley. There's not a lot to go on. The copy of the note the Critic left was examined and found to be the same as the one on the first vic. Both from the same typewriter and not from a computer printer, this guy is old fashioned. Forensics says he was murdered by blunt force and strung up for show. He was killed between 6 and 9 P.M. last night, hard to get a fix since it is freezing out there. Damn winter." Trapper turned pages in the folder and said, "Warren police are going over Ripley's apartment this morning so we will have more to look at." He read a bit more.

"The vic had plenty of cash and jewelry so this wasn't a robbery which we already figured, and he was missing a finger, the middle one of his right hand. Cut off cleanly, forensics says looks like maybe a branch cutter. I presume the Critic cut off his middle finger so he can give it to us." Trapper gave a little smile and closed the folder. He brought up another one from the floor where he dropped them and opened that saying, "Now our investigation of Andre Parker came up about as empty and the house was clean of prints. The security alarm was disabled, so the perp had to know about the set-up and which wires to cut. Parker's body was still tied to a chair in his kitchen and the machete was stuck through his chest, after the beheading, no prints on it. Guy must have been gloved."

Penny and Paula came to the door and asked if Trapper had her bodyguard, Trapper grinned and looked to Becker then back to Penny. "He's all yours."

Penny said, "Ok Barry, we girls want to do some shopping, come along. We're taking Paula's car." and they turned to go. Becker stood, gave a pained look and said to Trapper, "I'm not going to forgive you for this."

**

Chapter 12

As soon as the happy shoppers went out the door, Earl, Trapper and I burst out in laughter. "I'm really going to hate myself for subjecting Barry to that. He has to grow up sometime and learn the ropes. This job is not all glamour." Trapper grinned and sat back.

"He'll get over it. He'll only hate you for a week or two; especially after Penny drives him crazy dragging him around the stores. Now if we can get back to the Critic." I said.

Earl stood and said, "Sorry guys, but I have an investigation of my own. I got people to rouse and tell Paula I'll see her later." He went to his office as Trapper opened the file to another page.

"Okay, Ripley was hung with wire cable instead of rope, the forensic team thought that was a bit strange, considering rope is cheaper and easier to handle. The wire cable is the same as they use for cable TV in your home, so the killer may have cut it off someone's building or bought it in some store. Too many avenues to explore, and I don't have the man power to follow up on it. But no matter what he was hung with, it was just for show. He was killed by repeated blows to the back of the head with what Forensics says may have been a hammer, they found round flat impressions in his skull."

I reached over and took the copy of the note left on Ripley and read it again. "He says that he didn't like us trying to fool him with the cop. Now how could he know about Barry? He doesn't even look like a security guard let alone a cop. Has to be some one who knew what we were attempting, someone in your precinct or at the TV studio."

"Hell, only the Captain, Becker and I knew about it at the precinct. I'm sure the Captain hadn't told anyone, he didn't want the plan to backfire in his face. Now the studio, there was only a few people there who knew about this and had time to pull it off."

"Or let it slip to someone about it and they did it. Let's see, there was Joy, the guest scheduler, and the women who make-up Penny, the one's she jokingly refers to as her groupies and then Steve the floor manager. I don't think there was anyone else who could have known. I sure Penny wouldn't have told anyone."

"So we finish the taping at the studio, the killer waits for Ripley and murders him, then hangs him and goes over to put a note on your car just to piss us off. Sound about right to you?"

I just nodded thinking about the people at the studio who may be involved or may be a killer. I would rule out any one of the women, they wouldn't be able to put Ripley up to hang. Steve would be able to pull it off; he also would have access to wire cable. "I think we should talk to Steve at the station, care to go for a ride?"

I went to tell Earl but he had already left, I didn't even see him go. I guess due to all that subversive stealth governmental training he had he could disappear without our seeing. Trapper went to the door as I got on my cell phone and called Penny. She came on and it sounded like she was in a fight. "What are you into?" I asked.

"We're at a big close-out sale on designer dresses in the Image Boutique at the mall and there are a lot of women here fighting over dresses. Poor Becker, he doesn't know whether to run or arrest someone." She laughed.

"Great, you protect him. Trapper and I are going to your studio to talk to a few people but you have a key to let yourself back into the office, I'll see you later. Oh and don't get injured." I heard her yell something to Becker about grabbing a white strapless off the rack and she hung up.

"Barry is really going to hate you." I grinned and told Trapper what Penny had said, he laughed.

We drove out towards Penny's studio in my Crown Vic, it had been snowing most the morning, nothing serious just that light dusting to remind you that it's still winter. The freeway pavement was clear, the salt trucks had done their duty and we were making good time. I was going over in my mind the events since last Friday when they found the head of Parker. It really made no sense to kill people just because they weren't interesting enough to be on a talk show. Was there a hidden meaning in what was behind these killings?

Talk Show Murders

"You're unusually quiet." Trapper observed.

"Sorry, I was just wondering what the motive was for the killer. Why whack these people? They weren't anything life shaking, or threatening. What was the killer thinking as he did it?"

"Probably a guy who snapped after being forced to watch all the drivel on television. He just picked Penny's show to lash out. Kind of hard to get to Katie Couric and whack her."

"Yeah, but it isn't making sense to me. Parker was gay and off the wall; I can see him being killed, not that I would wish it on him. But Ripley was a man with a mission to clean up the world, why kill him?"

"Because the Critic couldn't get to Barry so he went for Ripley. Maybe." Trapper said.

"Yeah but Kepler did get to Barry and if we hadn't planted the GPS on him we may have lost him. Even if Kepler did say he was trying to protect him." I said.

"Speaking of Kepler, his alibi covered him; he was in detox all day in Detroit. So he's off the list as killer. Just a nut job with a warped agenda, he thought he was doing good."

"I'm sure Barry will appreciate that." I smiled. "Serial killers usually plan their kills carefully and usually stalk their prey before they kill. This guy didn't know from one day to the next who he's getting." I mused.

"Yep, crimes committed without premeditation. Doesn't excuse it, but makes it harder to solve. Do you think this could be because someone is trying to ruin Penny?"

"I thought about that last night when I couldn't sleep. Maybe someone has a grudge with Penny and wanted her to suffer by losing her show, which the station successfully took away from her. The battle with the networks is going on to see who has control over the show. Her ratings were up on the clouds and the network only sees dollars and not lives."

"Not to change the subject, but I will. How do you like working with Earl so far?" Trapper chuckled.

"I think it's going to be interesting. He's crazy, and will be useful as long as he doesn't bring in all his women to the office." I smiled as I watched the freeway wall passing by. We were in the "concrete ditch" portion of the freeway going south towards Penny's studio. I remembered the time we roared down this stretch chasing Penny's kidnappers during the classmate murders. Concrete on both sides of the below ground level freeway, only way out is walk or drive up one of the exit ramps.

"I first met Earl back in the academy out in Vegas, we shared a room and he was a wild man. In Vegas he had much to be wild about. We got along good and I kept him supplied with hookers." Trapper laughed at the memory.

We didn't get a chance to talk more about Earl as we arrived at the studio after getting off the freeway. We drove up to the gate and the guard saw me and yelled through my open window, "Sorry to hear they pulled Penny's show."

"Thanks, Harry, I'll tell her you mentioned it." He saluted and opened the gate arm. I parked and we had to go to the front entrance since I didn't have a passcard for the employee door. The receptionist looked up as Trapper and I walked past, she knew me. She expressed her disappointment in the cancellation of the show. I smiled, waved and went on.

We got to Gordy's office and found him on the phone. He waved us in and we sat. I thought about how Gordy knew the set-up, I whispered it to Trapper and he didn't say anything. Gordy finished his conversation and made a face. "The studio owners aren't yielding on the cancellation of the show, the network says since they are paying us for the show they should have a say in it. It's a mess but we'll get it straightened out soon. Now what can I do for you my friend?"

I asked, "Gordy, did you tell anyone about Barry Becker being on the show yesterday?"

Gordy thought for a minute, and then said, "I told our studio lawyer when he called to ask about our guest on the show. He needed to know if we were following the demands of the note. To protect our butts. He was all right with Barry since it was a sting operation. Unfortunately it didn't help much did it?"

"Well we got close, but not close enough. The killer knew about our plan so someone talked or someone inside did it. Now can you give us the name and address of the lawyer?" I looked to Trapper and said, "I would so love to take down a lawyer for the crimes."

**

Chapter 13

Earl walked up to the tiny brick building standing by itself on the short block just off the downtown of Auburn Heights. It looked old and had a Victorian trim around the front windows and had antique decorative architecture along the door and between the floors. There was a sign saying a dance studio was upstairs, not what Earl wanted. Earl was never crazy about this area of southeastern Michigan. It was just an odd mix of new and old and was in the shadow of the old Silverdome stadium that was sold to some foreign investors who wanted to turn it into a soccer stadium. Earl felt the only true football was the American football, not soccer.

The building he was approaching was a beauty salon called Lulu Loves Ladies. Earl had to chuckle to himself and imagined the place to be a lesbian bar. He entered the door and was struck by the ammonia and foul hair bleaching liquids that assaulted his sense of smell. The woman sitting in the first chair stood and said, "We don't generally do men's hair but I wouldn't mind running my hands through your hair." She was fairly attractive for a woman in her late fifties, Earl figured, and she had a bit of extra junk in the trunk as the brothers would say. "I'm Lulu, the owner, what can I do you for today?"

Earl went to her and held out his card, "Earl Daws, I'm a private investigator and I'd like to ask you a few questions about Margret McCoy." The woman just stared at Earl and sat back down in the styling chair, pointing Earl to a nearby chair by the front window.

"What do you want to know, we haven't seen her for a few days. I was worried that her bastard husband may have hurt her, but I didn't want to call to possibly start trouble at home."

"She's been missing for about four days and her husband hired me to find her." Earl said.

"He probably hired you because he didn't want the cops involved. They would have asked too many questions about their marriage." I thought that was a good possibility. She smiled like she had secrets.

"I ask questions too and I'm not restricted to being nice like the cops are. I go after my clients no matter who they are or what secrets they have." Earl said.

"I can see that, Magnum. What do you want to know?" She sat back and lit a cigarette. Earl eyed the cigarette and realized he hadn't had one since yesterday. She offered him one, but he figured he was doing well enough, why not stop. He declined and she threw the pack on the back bar knocking over a few bottles of goo.

"Can you tell me what you know about Margret and how was she as a worker?"

"Honey, she was a great little stylist. She could whip out a hairdo on most of these white haired women that shuffle in here. She was popular amongst the older crowd. As for her private life, Honey, this is a beauty salon so all secrets are told and gossip is a fact of life." She grinned and then said, "You want my opinion, if she's missing, look to her husband. He was real mean, came in here a couple times drunk and yelling about him not having any clean shirts or pants. I had to call the cops one time but he skittered out before they got here."

"Did they ever press charges for domestic assault or disturbing the peace?"

"Hell, no. Margret wouldn't press charges and the cops didn't see him in the act so they looked away. Besides, his old man is big around this city. He's a developer and has built most of the shopping centers and office buildings. Owns most of them too. City council loves him; he likes to contribute to their re-election campaigns. They wash each others hands, money for variances and permits."

"So junior survives because of his old man, any convictions for crimes?"

"Sure he's been in and out of Juvie and county since he was a kid. Real piece of work that one. Father always bailed him out or bought off a judge. Why a sweet gal like Margret ever got hooked up with him, I'll never know. But I think he knew how to push her buttons and since she was good looking, he went after her. She also said the sex was good too, a reason for staying in an abusive marriage. I'm no expert but she didn't think she was good enough for men. Mitch filled the need."

She spit out a bit of tobacco that came loose from her cigarette, Earl didn't find it attractive.

"Well, you have my card; call me if you hear any good gossip." He stood and shook her hand, she held on for a bit longer and smiled, "Anytime you want a trim, just stop in, even after hours." Earl felt a chill and thanked her, going out quickly.

He got into his car and drove off to his next stop, but he didn't see the car pull out from down the road after him.

~~*~~

Trapper and I found out from Gordy that Steve Handley, the stage manager had taken the day off since the show was canceled. I asked Gordy if he had an address for him and he called personnel to get it.

"You don't suspect Steve do you?" Gordy asked as he held out the paper with the address on.

"Not at this point, we just want to ask him a few questions, to see if he told anyone also. Thanks Gordy." We stood, "Penny's chewing nails on this cancellation, and I'm not sure how long she'll take it. I remember her contract says she can pull out anytime if her show is messed with. You think she may option that? We keep talking about Vegas, maybe there's a place for her out there?"

Talk Show Murders

"Come on Jim, I've been with Penny for five years now, please don't use the quit option on me, I didn't pull the plug. I'm behind her 100 percent. Blame the studio; they are the bad guys here." He said defensively.

"I'm sorry Gordy, I just hate seeing Penny the way she is and you're too handy to blame. Just pass the word about what I said to the big heads in the main office." I smiled and he said he would. Trapper and I went out to where Penny's show would have been taping, it was fairly empty. I looked around and then told Trapper that we should go find Steve.

We went back out to my car and I found Steve's home location on my Palm TX and we drove there, it wasn't far. I pulled into the drive and saw a Dodge Dart in front of the garage, I didn't know what kind of car he drove but at least someone was here. We went to the front door and rang the bell. A few minutes and a couple more rings, the door opened and there stood Steve looking a bit surprised.

"Hey Jim, and you're Trapper right?" Trapper said he was and Steve opened the door for us. "What can I do for you guys?"

We went into the house and he took us to the living room and asked us to sit. "We just needed to ask you a few questions about Kenneth Ripley and our man Barry. Did you tell anyone that they were going to be on the show yesterday?"

He looked a little surprised and said, "I didn't talk to anyone about them before the show or after the show. I didn't want to spoil your little trap. I heard about Ripley's death, it puzzles me. He was the type of guest that killer wanted, so why kill him?"

"We found out that the killer knew about Becker and our little ploy and we think he killed Ripley because of it. But our concern is how he knew Becker was a cop. No one said anything about it to anyone that we don't know about. You were one of a very few people in the studio who knew. We aren't accusing you, but want to know if you may have told anyone?"

"As I said, I told no one. It would be stupid of me to spread the facts of the sting." He sat back and smiled, I thought he answered honestly, but I could be wrong.

"So what are you going to do now that the show is on hold?" I asked.

"Mostly sit around, but I did want to start rewiring my entertainment center and the speakers throughout the house, so I have the time to putze with it now. I had cable television installed last week and I want to be able to watch it in any room of the house so I'm also stringing new cable into the other rooms from the entertainment center." He smiled.

I looked to Trapper and he looked back silently. "Are you stringing coaxial cable to do that?"

He said he was, I asked if we could see the cable and he made a strange face and stood, we followed him to a room down the hall and in. There was a spool of cable on the floor amongst a whole lot of wiring lying in different lengths. I picked up the end of the cable from the spool and looked at it. The markings along on the side of the cable were different than the cable used to string up Ripley, a different maker's name was printed. I showed Trapper and said, "It's not the same."

**

Chapter 14

Earl was heading into Auburn and was relaxing as he drove; listening to ZZ Top on the stereo and thinking about Paula's legs. He had a habit of glancing in his rear view mirror, from his days as an agent, to watch for tails. Traffic was very light so it was easy to see the blue Pontiac sedan following along as he went. Earl had a feeling and turned at the next side street, not knowing where it led, but wanted to see if the sedan followed, it did. Earl turned again on another side street and followed it around back to the main road. Before he went out to the main road he pulled into a parking lot of a Big Boy restaurant on that corner, and drove around the building coming back out to the front facing the sedan. Earl couldn't see the driver because of the heavy tint of the windows. The driver of the sedan must have seen Earl now facing him and drove back out of the lot onto the main road. Earl sped up and got on his tail, just before they came to a stop light at the next intersection. The light was now turning yellow so the sedan started to slow then suddenly sped up through the intersection just before it turned red. Earl had to stop, seeing as there was a cop car at the intersection getting ready to go. Earl didn't need any problems with the police out here.

Earl had noted the license plate number but it was partially covered by what looked like mud, so he only got the first four digits. He would call a buddy of his back in the Detroit police and would ask if he could trace it. He wondered how his people in the precinct were doing since he had walked out. He didn't care at this point about the job, just glad to be out of it. He missed a number of the men he had under his command and felt bad just leaving them like he did, he'd make up for it later. They were good men and would carry on without him.

Earl pulled out into the intersection when the light went to green and headed back the way he was going before the tail. Now why would someone want to tail him? Was there something more he should know about McCoy? It wasn't a cop car tailing him, and why would they? Well, Earl just had to find out, so he got the address of McCoy's home off of his address sheet and headed that way.

About ten minutes later he pulled into the drive of Mitch McCoy's rather elaborate home, family money he presumed. He parked and went to the door, just as it opened and out flew a surprised Mitch McCoy.

"Damn man, I was going to call you. Margret has been kidnapped!" He said in a loud voice and looked crazy-eyed.

"Whoa, hold up, when did you find this out?" Earl asked, grabbing the man's shoulders to steady him.

"About ten minutes ago, I got a phone call saying they had her. I called my dad and he said to get to his place where we could talk. I was just going there." He sounded a little calmer and took a big breath.

"Okay, I'm going to follow you, drive slow and careful." Earl let him go and went to his car as McCoy jumped into his Cadillac Seville and pulled out of the drive. Earl kept up with him as they drove out of town and up to a rather large wrought iron gate set back off the road. Earl could see

McCoy reach out to the call box and then the gate slowly opened to let them in. They drove up the long drive and Earl could see what money can buy, a very large house, no actually an estate, standing inside a ring of pine trees. They pulled up to the front entrance, a huge set of double doors, probably built so they get the concert piano through. Earl always felt uncomfortable around money people; they annoyed his sense of knowing there are poor people out there struggling.

The front left side of the door swung open and out stepped a tall, powerfully built man who looked to be in his seventies, but well preserved. Mitch ran up to him; Earl was expecting Mitch to genuflect before the man, but just stood looking like a scolded little kid.

The man gave an eye to Earl; Junior turned and quickly introduced Earl to his father. "Dad, this is the private investigator I hired, Earl Daws. Mr. Daws this is my father, Joseph McCoy."

McCoy Sr. turned his head to Daws and said, "Mr. Daws, welcome to our home, please come in, we have details to work out." He turned sharply like a solder in a parade and went in.

We went into a very elaborate library, book shelves filled with books from floor to ceiling on one whole wall. The room was filled with antique furnishings and a large ornate carved desk in the center of it all. On the desk was a mess of modern day apparatus, computers, printers, huge multi-monitors; a geeks wet dream.

McCoy Sr. pointed Earl to a chair and he sat. Mitch went to a straight back wooden chair that looked out of place in the fancy room, must be Mitch's punishment chair.

"Mr. Daws, my son has told me he hired you. Have you come across anything that can help us?" McCoy Sr. barked out.

"So far I've come across very little about your missing daughter-in-law and just now found out about the kidnapping." Earl looked to Mitch and asked, "What did the kidnappers say?"

Mitch looked to his father, who nodded, and said, "I got a call from someone saying they had Margret and wanted a half million dollars or she would be sent to me in little pieces. They said they'd call with the details and I should get the money together for when they call." He stopped and looked to the floor. Earl had enough training with the CIA to see that Mitch was withholding something or lying about the facts.

Joseph McCoy stood silently, and then turned to Earl. "I'm not a law enforcement person; I'm not sure what should be done. What do you suggest Mr. Daws?"

"Do you have the funds to meet the demand?"

"I do, I have that many times over, so it's no problem."

"Well, you should have it on hand just in case; if you delay they could do bodily harm to Margret." Earl turned his head to Mitch, "Did they say when they would call?"

"No, they just said they would."

"Did they call your home phone or cellphone?"

"My cellphone, I got it with me."

"It would be easy to track back the number that called you, if we have time."

"The caller ID said it was blocked." Mitch offered.

"There are ways to trace a number; I can make a call to have it done if you'll give me your phone."

Mitch pulled out his phone and handed it to Earl. He stood and asked if there was a private room he could go to make his call. Joseph pointed to a side room and said he could use that. Earl went to what looked like a lounge and stood just inside by the door listening to father and son. They were arguing about how Mitch could be so stupid to let this get out of hand. Mitch was defending himself saying he hadn't planned it to happen, they just had ideas of their own. They went quiet and Earl was suddenly aware that McCoy Sr. had approached the door; Earl grabbed his own phone and pretended to be talking to someone. McCoy Sr. smiled and went back to Mitch. Then Earl actually called a friend in the bureau and asked for a favor.

Earl came back in and said he had someone performing a check on the phone. He knew it would take longer than they had but noted Mitch's number to use later.

"I have a question, did either of you tell anyone that you hired me to find your wife?" Earl asked as he went to the window looking out at the expansive lawn. He looked back at Mitch and waited.

"I didn't tell anyone about it, nobody's business to know. Dad didn't know till I told him on the phone when I called about the kidnapping." Mitch said as he looked at his father for some sign of approval.

"Well, someone knew I was on this case, I was followed around earlier and possibly the last couple of days. Any idea who might want to follow me and why?"

Mitch looked sheepish and said, "Maybe the kidnappers?"

"How the hell would they know I was looking for her if neither of you told anyone? Also, if the kidnappers had her all this time why did they wait for almost four days to call, why not on the first day they had her?"

"Man, don't ask me, you're the detective, you find out why." Mitch whined.

"I intend to. Now I would suggest that you bring in the cops, they have the manpower and equipment to do the job, but I'm going to continue to find out what is going on with me being followed and why the kidnappers waited so long. The cops will only look to getting her back safely; I intend to find out who they are." Earl stood just watched their reactions, got none and he walked out.

**

Chapter 15

Trapper and I thanked Steve for taking the time to talk, we left and went to my car and sat for a moment. "The cable doesn't match, but that doesn't mean much, he could have had an extra piece that he used from another roll, maybe in his garage?" I said as we pulled out and away from Steve's home. I asked Trapper to get the address of the lawyer and he read it to me; I knew the area of Troy that the lawyer lived in, I had a friend who lived there years ago and I would go visit him every so often. We drove up Van Dyke to 16 Mile Road and then over to the street we were looking for. I drove down the block of very nicely manicured lawns and sculpted bushes, homes that just screamed money and I felt a dislike for lawyers even more.

We pulled into the drive and went up to the door, knocking several times to no avail. I was figuring that there was no one home when Trapper looked into the side window of the door and made a noise. He reared his foot up and kicked in the door as it blew open destroying the jam and trim. I was startled as he pulled his gun and looked to me nodding; I pulled my Glock and let him go in ahead of me. Down the hall I could see a man tied to the banister of the stairs going up to the second floor. The man had a very large knife sticking out of his chest, it was pinning a note to him. Trapper got on his cell phone and called his precinct to get Troy police to the address that he gave the person on the other end of the phone, saying it was a homicide with possible suspect still in the building, and then he hung up.

"I looked in the window and saw someone moving, and then I saw the body, be careful, he may still be in here." Trapper said quietly as he entered the kitchen. We saw that the back patio door was wide open and Trapper went to the door and looked out, he saw nothing. Trapper ran back into the building and then to the man who he checked for any sign of life, but the man was dead.

"I may not like lawyers, but this is no way to treat them." I said just as I could hear the sirens of the police arriving. This was a rich area and the police responded very quickly for these people. Trapper went out the front door holding his badge up for the approaching officer who had their guns drawn. The lead officer identified himself as patrolman Dave Bennet and asked what had happened as three other officers went into the building to look for anyone else. Trapper explained our reason for being there and how he found the body, chasing someone out the back door.

Officer Bennet got on his walkie-talkie and called for homicide. Trapper asked if Ralph Morton was still in Homicide and Bennet said he was, and probably would respond.

"I've said this before, you know just about every cop around metro Detroit don't you?" He grinned and went back into the house.

About an hour later and with frequent bull sessions between Trapper and Morton, they finally got the body off the rail and to a gurney, laying him on top of the opened black bag.

Trapper came over and told me, "The note on the body said that since the network wasn't going to do anything but re-runs, he was going to start taking it out on the people who work for the studio. The lawyer just happened to be on his list, this is going to get serious. He can make any demands he wants now, even if the network pulls the show he can claim he'll still murder until he gets the show put back on the way he wants it. Penny may still have a show to do soon." Morton called Trapper back and he went over leaving me alone, watching the coroner zip the body into the black bag.

I didn't like what Trapper had told me, and neither would Penny. As they were taking the body out to the meat wagon, my cell phone rang. I was expecting it to be Penny but it was Buck.

"Hey, what's up?" I asked.

"We're flying in tonight around 8:15 at Metro, can you pick us up since you dropped us off and we have no car?" He was talking loudly; there was a great deal of noise in the background.

"I can do that, same airline?"

"Yep, just reverse it all and we'll be there, later man, we're standing in the middle of traffic at McCarran Airport, going inside, so see you later."

He hung up before I could say anything and I pulled Trapper away from his walk down memory lane with Morton. I told him about Buck and that we needed to go back so I can get Penny ready for the ride to the airport and he can rescue Becker. He told Morton that he was leaving and to get him a copy of whatever he came up with and we left.

Bob Moats

We arrived back at the office and came in to find Becker holding up dresses for Penny and Paula to examine. They seemed happy and Penny came over to give me a kiss.

"We had a great time shopping. Paula has a great eye for fashions; she picked out some really fantastic clothes for us." She bubbled.

"Us? I hope you mean clothes for you and Paula." I asked cautiously.

"Of course, Sweetie, you'd look silly in a dress." She went over to Becker and took one of the dresses from him and put it in a bag.

Trapper went to Becker, "I hope you aren't sissified now. Got too much estrogen in your veins now. I want my bad boy Becker back."

Becker looked at him and smiled, "I had a mah-vellous time, pumpkin. You and I need to go shopping together one day."

Trapper smacked Becker on the back of the head and said to wise up. "We need to go follow up on a murder of the station's lawyer, so let's get with it."

Penny heard the remark and turned pale. "What are you talking about; did the Critic get Morty, our lawyer?"

Talk Show Murders

I went to Penny as she was looking panicky now and I put my arms around her, pulling her close, "Yes he was murdered earlier, we just got there too late to save him."

"Fuck! It's not going to stop is it?" She pulled her head back to look at me. "I want to get away from here, far away so the killer has no reason to go after these people. Let's get away please, so it will stop." She had tears in her eyes now. Paula pulled a tissue from the box on the desk and brought it to her, I thanked Paula.

"Running isn't going to help; he's reaching out to the network now, taunting them to his demands. He'll just keep up no matter where we are. So we'll stand and fight till he is caught." I said hoping it would help.

She put her head on my shoulder and took a big sigh. Trapper said quietly that he and Becker were leaving, Penny brought her head up and said with a small smile, "Thank you Barry, it was fun we'll have to do it again." They went out, Trapper saying he'd call me.

"Oh, we have to pick-up Buck and Maria at the airport tonight at 8:15, so we need to get going to be there on time." I said as Penny pulled away and went to the table with all their packages. She turned to Paula and said, "Welcome to our little family, it was a fun time and if you and Earl don't work out, well, I still want to be friends, okay?"

Paula went to Penny and gave her a hug and told her to hold up. Penny smiled and said she would.

"Earl told me to tell you he'd see you later, whenever that is." I said just as the door opened and Earl walked in. "Well, speak of the devil, and here he is."

"Hey you didn't have to all wait for me." He grinned and went to give Paula a big lip lock. "I actually missed you."

"Have any luck on your case?" I asked.

"Well the girl isn't just missing now, she's been kidnapped. I suspect that Mitch and now his old man had something to do with it, but I need to do more investigating." He said as he went into his office and looked out the window. I asked what he was looking for and he explained about the tail he had today.

"We can talk more tomorrow morning, I have to get Penny back home to take all her goodies, then we need to go pick-up Buck and Maria at the airport. I'm taking the limo to pick them up."

"The limo you got from the Traviano Mob family?" Earl asked.

"Yep, my prize possession now. Next to Penny." She whacked my arm and I corrected, "Second to Penny." She said better, put Willy in his purse and gathered her packages.

We said our good-byes and left. Earl turned to Paula as he locked the door and said, "I think I need a little dictation taken, are you in for it?"

She smiled and undid her belt and said, "Any dictation you need taken. I'm at your service."

**

Chapter 16

Penny and I had stopped at the house, dropped off her swag, fed Willy and breezed out the door. We went to a Burger King drive thru, grabbing the only food we had all day and ate our burgers on the way down to Metro Airport below Detroit.

"What happened today with Morty?" Penny asked and before I could answer she continued, "He was one of a very few lawyers who I thought was fairly straight. He negotiated my contract with the network for my show; I thought he was a good guy. He shouldn't have had this happen to him, not fair. He had nothing to do with the show."

I let Penny talk to get it out of her system, she told me how she first met Morty Kohn, the studio lawyer and how she didn't like him at first, but got along better as they got to know each other.

"So, what happened?" She asked again then went silent.

"He was stabbed and tied to his stairway with a note suck to his chest with the knife." Without even looking to her, I could tell Penny turned her head to the window. "Trapper and I arrived just as it was happening; the coroner said he hadn't been dead long. That rules out Steve Handley for the killing." I said more to myself.

"Steve, our floor manager? Why did you suspect him?"

"We weren't sure, but he did know that Barry was a cop and the killing of the agriculture man was because we had a cop on the show. Someone had to know or told someone. We talked to Steve asking if he may have told anyone about Becker, he said he told no one. We left him at his house and went straight to Morty's so Steve had no time to kill him, ruling him out."

"I'm glad because Steve is a good guy."

Trying to change the subject I asked, "So how was your day shopping with Barry and Paula." I could tell that brightened her up a bit.

Talk Show Murders

"I felt so sorry for Barry; he tried so hard to maintain his composure as we held dresses up to him to see how they looked. He was so quiet about it all especially at the Image Boutique where the women were going crazy over the clearance of high fashion dresses. I thought a couple of times he would pull his gun on some of the women. They were a bit over-zealous." She laughed, it sounded good to me. "Now Paula was a real surprise, she's not as dumb as she pretends to be. She has a B.A. and an M.B.A. all in business and she is very smart as I could tell from our conversations. She did let on that she was enjoying yanking Earl's chain about her being a bimbo. She does have a thing for Earl but she isn't in the market for a long term relationship. Her last and only marriage survived for twenty miserable years. Her ex was an executive at Parker Pharmaceuticals and made excellent money, but he couldn't get away from dipping his wick in the company secretary pool. Paula got a huge divorce settlement and can live comfortably for life. How much are you worth now?" She smiled.

"Enough that you could live comfortably for a couple years, but why do you care; you have three times the money I have?"

"A girl has to be concerned about her future. I think I'll keep you, there's more money to be made from your books." She gave me an evil little smile and just stared ahead.

Happily, freeway traffic was light and there was no snow on the roads; we arrived off I-75 and went into the airport in just under an hour from leaving home. We pulled into the parking structure and into the area for limos, then walked to the arrival gates of Southwestern Airlines and waited for Buck and Maria.

Penny was humming a tune to herself; I couldn't make out what it was. I finally couldn't take it and asked her. She smiled and said, "It's an old lullaby my mother used to sing to me, when I was not feeling well. I don't even remember the name or the words, just the melody. It always made me feel better." I kissed her cheek and suddenly saw Buck's bald head towering over the rest of the departing passengers coming out of the gate. He was alone.

"Hey big guy, where's Maria?" I asked as he got up to us.

"She got called back to work, seems the flu hit a few showgirls and they were calling the alternates back to fill in . She'll come out before winter ends to play in the snow." He beamed his huge smile and we went to get his luggage from the baggage carousel.

We were in the car heading back home and I was filling in Buck on what happened the past few days. He was sitting back in the limo enjoying the ride; Penny sat in the back with him. I felt like the chauffeur.

He kept saying ah-huh as I talked and then when I had finished he said, "Good thing I'm back, sounds like I'm needed here."

"I really want to be sure Penny is safe since this guy is killing indiscriminately now. I don't really think he would hurt Penny since it's her show that he wants to change but can't hurt to be careful."

"No mother trucker will get anywhere near Penny while I'm on the job." He smiled and Penny leaned over and gave him a kiss on the cheek. He sat back and just grinned.

We got to Buck's house and dropped him off. He said he would see us in the morning and I warned him about Paula. He said he would try not to scare her and went into his home. I drove us back to our home; Willy was sleeping on the front seat with his head up on Penny's leg. He looked so peaceful.

We got to the house and grabbed a couple of beers and chips and the three of us settled on the couch. "Here we are again, in our favorite place." I smiled and she kissed me.

Happily, Penny slept well that night, I didn't.

Next morning the phone rang about 6 A.M. and I rolled over to get it. I couldn't see the caller ID, so just answered. I mumbled hello into the mouthpiece and heard a voice whispering, "Good morning Jim Richards, is your lovely wife there?" I asked who this was as I swung out of the bed. "Never mind, I'll do the talking. Tell your wife that her show will be back on if the networks knows what's good for them." I looked to the caller ID and it said the call was blocked. "I'm not finished with killing people if your lovely wife doesn't do what I say."

"How the hell is she supposed to know who you approve of if you don't tell us? Who do you want to see on her show?"

"She'll just have to figure it out and no more games with the cops. I don't like to be messed with understand?" Then he hung up.

Penny was listening to my half of the conversation and sat up. "Is the bastard calling here now?" She demanded.

"I'm afraid so." I hung up and hit the number sequence for the call back feature but it didn't work. I figured he called on a cell phone, so the call back may not work. I took my cell phone and called Trapper who wasn't very happy to be woken so early. I explained what just happened and he said he'd get one of his men to check the phone records and would call me back. I hung up and stood turning to Penny and told her what he said.

"He won't tell us who he wants to see, how are we supposed to know?" She said as she got up and put on her robe.

"He did say you'd be back on the air, he must be doing something with the networks to get you back on." I said just as my cell phone rang, it was Buck.

"Hey Buck, what's up so early?" I asked, he said to turn on the morning news, any channel. I picked up the remote for the TV in the bed room and the local news was running with a recording of the same voice I heard on the phone earlier.

"This is to inform the CW Network and Station WFMD that if Penny Wickens' show isn't put back on the air by Thursday with the right guests, then I will kill one person a day till it is. I'll just pick random people now, maybe people from off the street, maybe someone in their home. Doesn't matter to me but it better matter to the television people. This is not an idle threat and to prove it, look in the dumpster of station WFMD for my first warning, that is all." The recording ended and the anchor person said, "The recording was received by our news people a half hour ago, and police have been informed as to the dumpster reference. We have a team of reporters going to WFMD as we speak and we will be going live as the breaking news happens."

I just shook my head and said, "Bloodthirsty bastards." Penny and I sat on the bed watching the scene unfold live and the camera crew was trying to get closer to the police scene but were held back. The camera person must have put a long lens on his camera that brought the dumpster in closer as police from Southfield were opening the top.

One officer yelled to get the ME, he said, "We got a body."

**

Chapter 17

I suddenly realized that Buck was still on the phone, I held it up and thanked him for calling and said we'd meet at the new office around 9, then I hung up. Penny was looking very bad, I took her and had her lie back down and told her to rest. My cell phone rang again and I went to answer, it was Trapper. I asked if he knew anything, he said it was going to take a little more time, the phone company won't release the info on the call without proper authorization, he said he was getting a warrant.

"Have you seen the news yet?" I asked.

Talk Show Murders

He said, "No, what's happening?" I went out to the living room and told him what had happened, I just heard him swear and he said he'd meet me at the precinct. He said it would be best to meet there because we'd need to coordinate with the other cities that had murders. I told him I was going to drop Penny off at the office so Buck can watch her and I would be in soon after. He said that was good and would see me later. We hung up and I went to get dressed. Penny was out of bed by the time I came back into the bedroom and she was getting dressed. I asked, "Are you all right now, or do you need to rest some more?"

"No, I'm good, I need to get out of here and get my head into this. You're going to go to see Trapper and work this out. I'm going to the office and sit with Paula and Buck and wait for something to happen." She sounded like she may still be a little out of it, but she looked to me and said, "I'm not going to let this all affect me, I'm all right and I want you to find the bastard and take him out." She said it low and seriously, and then went out of the bedroom. I finished dressing and went to the kitchen where I found Penny eating cereal and Willy was munching on his food.

I grabbed a fruit bar from the cookie jar and asked if she was ready to go out. She put her bowl in the sink, looked to me and said, "I'm ready."

Bob Moats

Earl was sitting in his office and Paula went to the door to unlock it, and then went to her desk. She and Earl had just gotten back from her place where they showered and changed clothes, well, Paula had changed, Earl had an extra shirt at the office for emergencies but he knew he'd have to go to his place eventually for a complete change. They were relaxing when Buck walked in around 8:30 and Paula looked up from her desk, got wide-eyed at the big man and asked if she could help him. Buck gave her his trademark smile and said, "You must be Paula."

Earl came out of his office when he saw Buck in the vestibule, opened the door and they high-fived and shook hands. Earl introduced Buck to Paula and then they went to the round table to sit and talk. They were telling Paula about how they met and their adventures, and then Buck filled Earl in on the murder this morning, just as Penny and I walked in.

"Nice to see everybody relaxing," I said. Penny went over as Paula stood and they hugged, it gave me a slight tingle to see two gorgeous women embrace. I had to get my head back to reality. "I suppose Buck filled you in on the killing this morning?" I asked Earl.

"Yea, this is getting bad, I'm going to see if I can work out my case as soon as possible to help you guys out. I know Trapper can't handle the stress too well, so he'll need me." He grinned widely and then his phone rang, he excused himself and went to his office. Penny and Paula were sitting by the reception desk talking and I went to Buck, "Thanks again for coming back, sorry about Maria not making it."

"Yeah, she was just about ready to go with me and got the call. She's a trooper, wouldn't let the show down so she stayed. She'll be out when everyone is well again. Now you want me to hang in here and watch these two beautiful women? A delightful job if you ask me." He grinned.

Earl came out and sat, smiling, "I called a buddy of mine in the bureau and he checked the phone call from the kidnappers, it came from a throwaway phone, no way to trace it. But the good news is, I had him run the financials on my client and his father, seems McCoy Sr. is in debt up to his ears. He told me yesterday that he could come up with the half million for the kidnapping, but seems he's going to be a little shy of covering the payment. I'll need to check if Margret had a big life insurance policy and if there was a plot to have her come up dead to collect it."

"The plot thickens," I said as my cell phone rang, it was Trapper. "Yea chief, I'm listening... Okay, I'll be there." I hung up and said, "Trapper has homicide detectives from five cities meeting at 10 to see if we come up with a plan to catch the Critic. He got hold of reps from the studio and they are coming in also." I said that more to Penny than anyone else. I stood and told Buck not to get too bored and gave my apologies for leaving and departed.

Earl gave Paula a big wet one and said there was crime out there to fight and said he'd be back later. Paula looked to Penny after he went out and laughed, saying that Earl is a big teddy bear for such a macho man. Buck went to turn on the huge LCD TV that hung on the wall and found a rerun of the Beverly Hillbillies. He plopped on the couch and said, "We are digging in for the duration, I am on the job." He had his nickel plated .38, tucked in front under his belt; he gave his big smile and relaxed. Penny and Paula went into Earl's office and sat gossiping.

I arrived at the Clinton Township police precinct and was told to go right into Trapper's office. There were four men seated, representing cops from Detroit, Troy, Sterling Heights, Madison Heights and soon a couple more towns. Trapper said that we should go to a conference room before we packed his office. We were heading that way when Captain Barrows came out of his office and walked with Trapper to the room. After about ten minutes of waiting two more cops arrived then the studio rep was brought in.

Trapper spoke, "Gentlemen, we have a problem. The Critic, as we have started calling him, has threatened to start murdering indiscriminately in our cities. The death this morning was of a man from Allen Park who was on his way to work, according to his wife. He didn't have any connection to Penny's show or the studio. So it is now a metro Detroit wide problem." He looked to the studio rep and asked. "What is WFMD's position on this now?"

The man looked uncomfortable being surrounded by cops and stood, "Uh, my name is Larry Lang, I have talked to the owners of the station and we will give our cooperation to the police in this matter and whatever is in the best interest of the viewers. They don't want anymore murders on their conscience."

"Or poor ratings." a homicide Lieutenant from Madison Heights joked. Everyone laughed then Trapper asked for some respect. They all got serious and Captain Barrows spoke now.

"Gentlemen, we need answers and facts. Why is the Critic doing this, and what is his plan. We need to dig into the station's employee list to see if it could be coming from within. We need to read every complaint the station has received in the last couple years to see if a disgruntled viewer has slipped his gears. All patrol officers need to be on alert for anything out of the ordinary. We need to assign as many men to this as possible, but we need to be discreet, he can kill at anytime if he knows we are making an all out manhunt for him. Let's be careful who we talk to and what we ask. Is this good with everyone?" They all nodded and then he continued, "I'd appreciate it if everyone can give Trapper the lead command on this, to coordinate the attack, is that agreeable?"

They all agreed again and then Trapper introduced me to them as Penny's husband and a private investigator with a good background in serial killers. Most the men knew my name when Trapper mentioned it and they all nodded to me. "Jim is a now a civilian consultant with us, he has the inside track on the studio and what his wife's involvement with this criminal may be. So please give him that respect."

Trapper spent a few minutes asking what everyone could provide in the way of help, they all gave their support and talked about what they would do. It was a plan but I felt it wasn't going to be enough. This guy was dangerous and may need to be dealt with one on one.

For Penny's sake and sanity, I would step up to that task.

**

Chapter 18

All the cops had departed along with the station rep, after he told Trapper and me that the station was going to be putting Penny back on the air. They just had to figure out how to get guests;

most people were turning them down. He left and I sat with Trapper back in his office.

"Let's go back over this," I said, "the first killing of Parker occurred just after the show at his own house. The killer would have had to know where Parker lived and when he'd be home. He took the time to kill Parker, package up his head, drop it here at the precinct and get lost. With me so far?" Trapper nodded as I continued, "Then we plant Becker on the show and the Critic goes after the agriculture guy, while we watch the wrong person. So the Critic had to also know where he lived and kill him, take his body to the park and string him up. Still with me?" Trapper was looking annoyed now and said he was. "The station pulls Penny's show and he kills the lawyer. Now how would any one person know who Morty was and that he was the station's lawyer? And why him? I'm really thinking that the Critic is someone in the station and has access to all this information. The random killing this morning may have been to throw us off, he may have figured he was getting careless."

"So before you ask me again if I'm with you, I think we need to take a ride to the station and start questioning people, are you with me so far?" Trapper asked with a smirk on his face.

"Yeah, I'm with you, shall we go?" I grinned. We left his office, went out to his unmarked car and drove out to WFMD.

Bob Moats

~~*~~

Earl was driving along enjoying Robert Palmer's "Addicted to Love" on the disk player in the car when he looked back in his rear view mirror and could see that the dark blue Pontiac was still there. He had spotted the tail about five miles back and was seeing how far it would go. Earl cruised up Stephenson Highway heading to McCoy Sr.'s house after he called from his cell phone to be sure someone was there. Joe McCoy said he had the cash when Earl ask him and said the police would be informed after they found out if Margret was still alive. Otherwise they weren't paying a cent. Earl had to chuckle when McCoy said that, knowing Joe didn't have that much cash, he probably padded the money with newspaper.

Earl was taking the long way round to McCoy's home just to annoy the tail and get him relaxed enough to make a mistake. Earl drove up Stephenson Highway until it turned into Rochester Road then got just past East Auburn Road when he turned into an abandoned gas station and drove around the side. The Pontiac approached slowly and came around the side of the building when Earl rushed up to the driver's door from behind the Pontiac and pulled the door open.

Earl reached in to pull the driver out but found a 9mm Glock stuck in his face. Earl had his gun low in the driver's side and it looked like a stand off. Earl slowly backed away from the car as the driver got out still pointing his gun at Earl. The driver slowly reached in the cheap jacket he was wearing and pulled out a flat wallet and flipped it open, holding it up for Earl to see.

Even at a distance of six feet, Earl recognized the badge as FBI. He moved slowly closer as the man held it out for him to see. Earl was reading the name on the ID and smiled. He stepped back and asked, "You know Lenny Krujenkins?"

"Yeah, the biggest fuck-up in FBI history." The driver was now smiling and lowered his weapon, so did Earl, but they both kept hold of the guns. The driver asked, "You worked for the bureau?"

"Nope CIA, Washington, late sixties, Intelligence. But I knew a lot of guys in the D.C. bureau to know about the legendary Krujenkins." Earl put his gun in its holster, so did the driver.

Earl held out his hand to shake and said, "Earl Daws and why have you been tailing me."

"Mark Gaitlin, just seeing if you are getting anything on McCoy." The man smiled. "We've had him under surveillance for the last two weeks when we figured he was ripping off the government by building crappy offices with below sub-standard materials and charging the government full price."

"How'd you know to follow me, or that I was involved with the McCoys?"

"We also had his idiot son's phone tapped and he told us when he hired you. We checked you out and hoped you may lead us to something. I'm just one small part of the operation, we have others watching his house and following the kid. I got assigned to you."

"I hope I didn't disappoint you."

"No, but you surprised the crap out of me when you caught me yesterday with that stunt around the Big Boy. I changed cars today and should have learned when you pulled in here. Well now you know, I hope we can work together on this?"

Earl grinned and said, "I'm always available to help our government save a few dollars. Tell me what you know."

~~*~~

Trapper and I arrived at the station and found Gordy in his office. He looked a little frazzled and said to come in, we did.

"Gordy, can you put us in touch with someone here in personnel who can help us go over the employee list?" I asked.

"Sure Jim, hang on." He picked up his phone and punched a few buttons and talked to someone named Francine. He asked if Penny's husband and a police officer could come over and snoop through the employee files. He listened and then smiled, hanging up he said she'd be waiting. I took Earl to the personnel office and we found Francine sitting all alone at a very small desk surrounded by file cabinets. She smiled and held out her hand, I took and gently shook it.

"So you are the famous detective married to our gal Penny?" she asked.

"Yep, that's me, Mr. Wickens." I smiled back.

"So what do you want to know from my files?"

"We're going to try and narrow down a few people who had access to the people who were murdered this last week. Mind if we sit and brainstorm?" I asked.

"No, have a seat and go to it, ask me if you need anything specific, I know where most of the people are in the system."

"Thanks," I answered and nodded Trapper over to a couple of chairs around a small table, we went to sit.

"Okay, Sherlock, now what?" Trapper asked. I took a piece of paper from a small pile on the table and started to write names on it of people who knew who the guests were.

"Okay, Penny, me, Steve, Gordy, Joy from scheduling and no one else I can think of. Great place to start." I sat back and thought hard on who else was in on knowing the guests and our involvement with Becker.

Francine called someone on the phone and shortly a young man came in and took a folder Francine handed him and went off with it. I asked Francine who he was and where he was going. She told me he was a mail boy and a runner when they needed something delivered internally.

I leaned forward and said to Trapper, "I remember a runner taking Barry's information to Steve the other day. He would have known about the ruse and maybe someone to look at."

Trapper said, "Yeah, I remember the guy you're talking about, but this kid wasn't him." Trapper turned to Francine and asked, "Is there more than one runner in the building?"

"Sure, there's about six of them, with all the paperwork that goes through this place, they are busy." She replied.

I asked, "Where do they start from, their office I mean?"

"Down the hall from here on the right, it's the mail room, can't miss it."

Talk Show Murders

I thanked her and we went out, down the hall and into the mail room, where we found three young men sorting mail. Trapper said none of them looked like the guy from the other day. One of the men saw us and came over, "May I help you?" he asked. Trapper flashed his badge and asked if they were all of the people who worked in the mail room?

"There's the three of us and two out on runs, and one who is off sick. Oh, here's the other two now." He said as two more young men came in the room. Trapper checked them and said to me they weren't the one.

"You said there was one other who is off sick?" I asked.

"Yes, that's Norm Perkins, he's kind of a goof-off, always calling in sick or leaving early for stupid reasons."

"Can you describe him?" Trapper asked.

"I can do better; he left his photo ID badge." The man went to the wall and took the thing off a hook and showed it to us. There was a photo of the guy, Trapper said that was him.

"Gee, a guy who comes and goes when he wants, has access to addresses, knows what guests are on and what people are connected to the station, are you with me so far?" I grinned.

"About as far as I can throw you." Trapper snarled and asked the guy if he had an address for Norm. "We need to go see our missing mail boy."

**

Chapter 19

The mail guy gave us Norm's address and phone number, and then Trapper asked, "Tell me about this Norm Perkins, what kind of person is he?"

"Besides a jerk, he's a lousy worker and I'm certain he lied a lot."

"Glowing appraisal, is he nosy or asks a lot of questions about the guests?" I asked.

The man made a face and said, "Yeah, he was always hanging around Joy in scheduling, hoping to get the easy runs to the studio so he could watch the shows being taped. Then he would return and complain about the way they did things. I think he wanted to run the shows himself because all he did was criticize everything."

I looked to Trapper and smiled. "Shall we go find our little critic?"

Talk Show Murders

Trapper asked if we could keep the ID badge to copy the photo, the man said he couldn't see why not, Norm never used it. Trapper put it in his pocket and we went out to our car. I was navigating to Paul's house and when we arrived Trapper had already called for back-up from the Warren police since we were in their town. He also had called Captain Barrows and explained the whole thing and our suspicions, the Captain said he would see if he could get a quick warrant and hung up. We waited down the street from Perkin's house as the Warren cops pulled up. Trapper greeted an old friend of his from Warren homicide, Detective Ken Morgan, and they were talking when the call came in. Trapper answered, listened and said Barrows found a judge who happened to have had Morty as a friend and wished us luck. We waited for the warrant to arrive; Morgan had officers around the back now watching for Perkins to slip out. A car pulled up and the driver handed Trapper the warrant and Trapper yelled we're good to go.

Everyone converged on the house with Trapper and Morgan going to the door banging and yelling to open up. No answer, Morgan signaled to his man to bring the ram up just before trying the door to see if it was open, the door wasn't locked. Morgan looked surprised and said to Trapper, "Either it's a trap or the guy trusts people." He signaled his men and everyone filed in. The place was empty of anyone.

We took our time searching the place and Trapper said to look for loose coaxial cable. After a few minutes of searching one officer came up with a spool of wire, Trapper called for me and I looked at it. "Same manufacturer as the wire that hung Ripley in the park. I'd say that forensics should be able to match the cuts on this to the one they have in evidence. We now know our killer."

Trapper said to me he needed to get Perkin's picture ID badge to his lab to have blow-ups made and get them out to all cops in the area. I found on a desk a larger picture of Perkins and some girl and gave it to Trapper. "They can blow them up and put them both out." I said.

Morgan said he was going to assign a couple cars in the area to watch for Perkins if he comes back. Trapper said to clear everyone out and put everything back the best they could to make it look like they hadn't been there. We all went out and to our cars; Morgan went to assign a couple officers to watch the house and to yell if he came back. They would get copies of his photos coming through the computers in the cars. Trapper and I left the scene and headed back to his precinct.

~~*~~

Earl was sitting on a folding chair in the "command center" of the rented house just down the street from McCoy Sr.'s home. The house was odd in that it was an older and more dilapidated home than the rest of the neighborhood. It looked to have been built years before the rich people built their mini-mansions and moved in. Agent Gaitlin brought Earl a styrofoam cup of coffee and sat next to him.

"Any word on the kidnapping?" Earl asked.

Gaitlin gave an odd look to Earl and said, "What kidnapping?"

"Haven't you been tapping the phones? The wife of Mitch McCoy was kidnapped."

"News to us, they haven't said anything on the house phones we have tapped. They must be using burn phones; did they call you from their home or cell?"

Earl pulled out his cell phone and checked the caller log. He showed it to Gaitlin and the agent yelled over to another agent with headphones on as to what number they were hooked to. The agent called out the number and they saw it wasn't the number on Earl's phone. He asked the tech if they could do a trace on the number and he said he'd try.

"So you were hired to find the missing wife, which we knew, but now it turns up as a kidnapping?" Gaitlin asked.

"Yea and I'm starting to wonder if the wife is still alive. Or did they make up the kidnapping to bring out the body earlier than waiting years for a missing person to be presumed dead? Okay, the idiot son calls me to set up the missing wife, then I scout around and come up with nothing but people saying that hubby could have killed her. Then I arrive just as the son is screaming about kidnapping and we go to daddy's home to bring the plot to a boil. They don't know I checked on their financial situation and found out they are broke. If they just made Margret disappear, they wouldn't be able to collect any insurance right away. Which I still have to check on to see if she had insurance, but I'll bet it was for a lot."

Gaitlin held up his hand and called to another man and had Earl give him the particulars of the woman so they could check on any insurance. Earl gave the man his info and then continued. "So daddy says he has the cash, but doesn't, and then they will stage the drop and the girl will be found dead anyway, they can now collect the insurance post haste. They are off the hook for murder, it was the kidnappers. But what I don't understand is if McCoy is ripping off the government for millions, why are they broke?"

"That's what we're trying to figure out. The money has been transferred and paid to McCoy, but our people have also found that he is broke, we need to know where he has stashed the money or who he has given it to."

139

Talk Show Murders

"You thinking he's funding some terrorist cell or some good old boys network to take over the government?" Earl smiled.

"That's why we're spending taxpayers' dollars to watch him." Gaitlin sat back and grinned.

"You'd think the Feds would spend a few more dollars on good coffee." Earl grimaced as he took another sip from the cup.

~~*~~

Penny had just raised Buck a dime and Paula folded. Buck watched Penny closely, remembering the poker game on the cruise when Penny had beaten all the men and made them all get facials the next morning. Buck didn't want to admit it but the facial felt good. Buck couldn't see Penny giving any tells and called the dime and dropped his cards. Penny dropped hers and won.

"Damn it's good we're not playing strip poker, I'd be butt naked by now." Buck groaned. Penny laughed and gathered the small change that was on the table. Paula went to make some more coffee, just as the door opened and in walked a man around his late twenties, medium height and stockily built. He looked to have lifted weights. Buck had his hand on his revolver as Paula went to the desk and slid open the reception window to talk to the man.

"May I help you?" She asked.

He looked through the glass separating him from the main room where Penny and Buck still sat at the round table, then turned to Paula and said quietly, "I was wondering if Mr. Richards is in?"

Paula smiled and said, "He's out on a case and Mr. Daws is also out, can I take a message or schedule an appointment for you?"

"No, I'll come back, when is a good time?"

"Usually early in the mornings is when you can catch them. Do you need an investigation?"

"Oh, it's just a small thing, I need someone found, I'll come back." He had a strange smile on his face, like he was thinking something that he wasn't saying. "I can return tomorrow morning to see Mr. Richards."

"Would you like to leave your name and a way he could reach you?" Paula was pushing.

"No, I'll just come back, thank you." He looked back to Buck and Penny again and went out. Paula snorted and said that was odd.

Penny was having a strange feeling that she had seen the man before but he wasn't really that familiar to her. Paula finished the coffee and they played another hand of poker when I came in without Trapper. He stayed at the precinct to follow up on Perkins and get the word out. They had made copies of the pictures and he was going to distribute them everywhere he could. I came through the vestibule door and Paula said I had just missed a man needing help.

"I'm a little tied up right now to take on any more cases." I kissed Penny and peeked at her hand. I said to Buck, "Fold now while you still have your money." Penny whacked me.

"Well you'll be happy to know we have identified our Critic." I announced and turned to Penny. "He works at your station and his name is Norm Perkins."

I heard Penny take a big breath and made a small noise, I asked, "What's the matter?"

She was pale and turned her head to me and said, "I thought he looked familiar, Norm Perkins was just here."

**

Chapter 20

I told Buck to watch the women and I went out the door with my Glock in hand. I carefully went out the building entrance and looked towards the parking lot. Nothing was moving. I made a sweep around the building and came back around to the front. He was long gone. I pulled out my cell phone and called Trapper and told him what had just happened.

"Either Perkins doesn't know that we know it's him or he does and he's taunting us now. I'm going for the fact he doesn't know. He's sizing us up for something, maybe an attack on one of Penny's friends, like Buck or Paula now. Or even me. He still wouldn't hurt Penny, he needs her for the show. I'm keeping Buck close by now and Earl should decide what to do about Paula. We got to take this bastard down Will. I'm getting tired of nut cases picking on Penny."

Trapper told me on the phone, "I called the studio and warned the mail room guys to keep mum about us asking about Perkins, they all agreed to not say anything, especially when I threatened them with arrest. If he goes back to work, I asked them to go to another area of the station and call me so we can get there to nab him. I hope he doesn't know we're on to him yet, he could get lost in the wind."

"Well, we know who he is now, shouldn't be too hard to find him with his picture out there. Maybe you could post it on the news to get people involved in finding him."

"Yeah, but that can end up in a witch hunt and every poor slob who looks like Perkins may get mobbed and beaten." Trapper replied.

"True, hey I just had a thought." I said.

"Hope it didn't hurt." Trapper replied.

"Remember Anthony Perkins from the movie 'Psycho'?"

"Yeah, what about him?"

"Anthony Perkins played Norman Bates, the psycho killer. Our man is named Norman Perkins." I smiled. "Just a piece of stupid trivia."

"Yes, stupid but scary. Maybe he was scarred for life after seeing the movie."

"I'll be careful when I take a shower." I laughed.

"I have to go, the Captain just breezed by and signaled me, you watch out for this guy." Trapper said then hung up.

I went back into the building and my office, the three of my friends were sitting in Earl's office with Buck by the door. He stood and came out, "I presume you didn't find him, I heard no gunfire."

"Nope, he was gone. I called Trapper to tell him. Can you stay at our place tonight just for insurance?"

"I can indeed, I'd love to." He replied.

Penny came out the door and asked, "What about Paula?"

"I'm sure Earl can watch her just in case Perkins goes after her. I'll call him and fill him in on the new developments."

~~*~~

Earl was standing in the driveway of the FBI's rented house getting ready to go see what the McCoy's had in store for him, when his cell phone rang. It was me. I told him about finding the identity of the Critic and he was glad we had a lead. I also told him about Perkins visit to our office, he didn't like that.

"He's gotten a look at the layout of the place and saw Buck, Penny and Paula, not good. I don't know how long I'll be on this sting so if you could be sure Paula is safe until I can get to her, I'd appreciate it."

Talk Show Murders

He explained his case to me and I said it's good the FBI is involved, that way he wouldn't get killed. He made an obscene comment and hung up. Earl turned to see Gaitlin coming out of the house and approach him.

"McCoy was just on the phone talking to some guy named Dominic Russo, we ran him and he has connections to a minor crime family in Ohio. We get the feeling that Russo doesn't have the girl, but some good news, or bad for Margret, we ran a check and she is insured for two million dollars. Sounds like a plot to me."

"So the McCoy's will make the drop of the phony money and then her body turns up dead, insurance company has to pay, maybe more if McCoy can claim accidental death by murder. They get the money but where does that go from there? Are they keeping the cash or moving it to where ever they put their money." Earl went quiet and looked to the house, thinking.

Gaitlin spoke, "Whatever they pull we need something on them, do you mind being wired?"

Earl said that was good with him so they both went back into the house and Earl got wired for his meet.

About a half hour later, Earl arrived at McCoy Sr.'s house and went to the door just as it opened.

Mitch was standing in the doorway and asked, "What took you so long?"

"I had to shake that tail you said you didn't know anything about. I'm getting tired of being jerked around, let's get this over." Mitch was giving Earl a dirty look and had him come in. They went to the same room as before and Joseph McCoy was seated at the desk now with a large satchel in front of him. Earl went to the desk and stood waiting.

"The kidnappers have called again and want someone to bring the money to them. They said they didn't want my son or I to do this, they wanted a neutral person to deliver the cash. I hope you will earn your fee and do the drop?" Joseph asked.

Earl figured that they would want him to do the drop, that would make it look like they had nothing to do with it, to disassociate themselves from the murder. Earl decided to make a play; he made a smirk and sat in a chair by the desk.

"The plan sounds all right, but there is going to be a small change in the program." Earl reached over and grabbed the satchel and Joseph tried to grab it back but Earl was quick. Earl opened the satchel and pulled out a stack of bills, flipping through and finding most of it was newspaper. Earl threw the stack at McCoy.

"I'm no dummy guys, I did some checking on you and it seems, Joe, that you are not exactly rolling in dough. In fact you're about broke. I also did some checking and find that your daughter-in-law was insured for two million dollars. Gee, it would be too bad if she came up dead by the kidnappers wouldn't it. All that insurance money going to Junior here. I want in on your little scheme."

McCoy looked to his son and said, "Dumb shit, you had to pick a crooked P.I. didn't you? Always making stupid mistakes, like the jerks you hired to grab Margret." He went silent, then turned to Earl. "So, what do you want out of this?"

"Okay, you hire some goons to grab Margret, then stage a fake kidnapping to divert attention away from the fact that your intention was to murder her for the insurance money. I get all that, not a bad plan. But why all this trouble? You had millions from your scam with the government, did you loose all that cash in the stock market or gamble it a way?"

"It seems, Mr. Daws, you are well informed, I had millions, yes, but as one crook to another you know that there are bad deals made and I made a few. I got involved with some people who had found out about my swindling the government out of money by using sub-standard materials in the buildings I was constructing for them. They had some invoices showing where I was getting the materials and they would bring it to the attention of the right people if I didn't pay them off. I went broke trying to get them off my back and buying back the invoices. I needed the cash now to keep my business going and I came up with this plan."

"So is Margret still alive or have they done her in already?"

"I have no idea, the goons my son hired have her and they aren't talking. They want the money even though they don't know I'm broke, they think it's all for show to hide my funds from the government, but they got greedy and wanted the cash also. I seem to make poor choices of who to trust haven't I Mr. Daws?"

"Yes, you have. Do you know where they are holding Margret?"

"I'm not sure, but they said they were close and the drop is to be held at noon today in back of the old movie theatre in downtown Auburn. You were to drop the case in a dumpster behind the theatre and leave. They would then call as to where she was."

"Or where the body was. They don't know that you are sending bogus bills do they? It was your intention that they kill her in retaliation for deceiving them, but they could still finger you for the set-up."

"What, the word of a couple of kidnapping murderers, against the word of a prominent businessman? I'm not worrying."

Joseph went silent, Mitch didn't have much to say either. Earl just shook his head and said to the wire, "Is that enough for you, Gaitlin?"

He could hear the front door open and in swarmed FBI agents all ready to do battle, but the McCoy's just sat. Earl felt kind of sorry for them, they really were losers.

**

Chapter 21

Earl stood out back of the dilapidated movie theatre, holding the now empty bag. He looked around and could see no vantage point from where he could be spied on to see if he dropped the bag in the dumpster. He figured the thugs would just trust him to drop the bag off at the appointed time and then walk away. Earl lifted the cover of the dumpster and dropped the bag in.

About fifteen minutes later a shadowy figure came down the alley to the back of the theatre and around the corner to the dumpster; lifting the cover he expected to see a bag in the trash but found a gun in his face. Earl grabbed the man by the collar and vaulted over the side of the dumpster and pushed the man to the ground, placing cuffs on him. Earl yelled to the door at the back of the theatre and out came Gaitlin and a couple other agents.

Earl pulled the man up and got close to his face, "Okay douche bag, where is the girl and she better be alive!" He yelled in the man's ear. The man said nothing. Earl swung the man around and threw him into the wall of the theatre, causing the man to expel the air in his lungs and drop to the ground.

Gaitlin picked the man up and quietly said to him, "You better talk or my friend will help you to speak. He's a trained torturer, having spent a number of years in Guantanamo helping to waterboard a few bad guys. Understand me, asswipe?"

The man looked scared but still was silent. Earl came to the two men and said to Gaitlin, "Why don't you and your agents go have a smoke, while I discuss the problem with our friend." Gaitlin smiled and told his men to follow him as they went around the corner of the building. Earl pulled the now shaking man to the side of the dumpster and all that was heard for the next few minutes was a few muffled screams and then silence. There was a brief conversation and Earl pulled the man back out and yelled for Gaitlin. The agents went to take the man as Gaitlin and Earl stood waiting for them to go.

"Well, I got an address, are you with me?" Earl asked.

Gaitlin nodded and they went to Earl's car and drove out to the end of town to a house that was back off the road. Earl parked at the shoulder of the road away from the front of the house and they sat watching the house. "We can do this quiet, or we can storm the place." Earl asked.

"I can have a team of agents here in five minutes." Gaitlin offered.

"Nah, too many people and the girl will be dead. Let's do this quietly."

The two men went up the side of the property and over to the house, sitting under the only window on that side of the house. Earl made a cautious peek into window, he could see through the bedroom door out into the living room. He sat back down and quietly said, "I can see her tied to a chair. We need to draw out the men so we can separate them. Want to flip as to who draws them out?"

"I have a better idea." Gaitlin said, and went to the back of the property and took a gas can by a lawn mower that he saw as they came up to the house. He picked up a bottle lying in the uncut grass and brought it back to Earl, they carefully filled the bottle about halfway and stuck a rag he found into the neck and then lit the rag. Gaitlin ran to the front side of the house and tossed it at the car in the drive, the bottle made contact with the car, broke open and the gas was now flaming. Earl threw a stone at the front window hoping to make the men inside notice the car. It worked, three men came running out and danced around trying to figure out what to do. One man ran to get the garden hose at the front of the building and tried extinguish the fire.

All this time Earl had gone around the back and carefully broke the glass window from the back door and opened it. He went in with his gun pointed ahead and found the girl in the living room, alone. Earl pulled out his pocket knife and cut the girl's bonds and took her to the back door and out. He had her go hide behind a small shed that was out back and he ran up the side to join Gaitlin.

"I know if we jump them, they'll start shooting and we'll have to shoot them back. You ready to bust some butt?" Earl smiled.

Earl and Gaitlin came around the side yelling to freeze, the bad guys all pulled their guns but Earl and Gaitlin had the drop. Earl took out the two on his right and Gaitlin shot the gun arm of the other stopping him cold. Earl looked to Gaitlin, as Gaitlin said, "We need one good witness alive to testify to McCoy's crime."

Talk Show Murders

About ten minutes later the place was crawling with Feds and they found that one of the men Earl shot was still alive. Margret was telling Gaitlin and Earl her story of how she was taken with Mitch's blessing. She was pissed.

They drove her back to the rental house and she gave her official statement to the agents. Both the McCoys were handcuffed to chairs in the living room until they would be taken to a Federal processing station for accessory to kidnaping and defrauding the government. They would be away for a long time.

Margret came over to Mitch and slapped him hard with her right hand nearly knocking him off his chair, then spit in his face. "You son-of-a-bitch, I hope you fry in hell, and I will have everything you own in the divorce I'm going to start." She spit again and walked away.

Earl had called her parents and they showed up shortly after to take their daughter away from there. Gaitlin told Margret that she would be needed to testify against the McCoy's and she said it would be her pleasure.

Earl went to Gaitlin and asked if he was needed anymore. Gaitlin said, "Oh think we can handle it from here. I appreciate the help you gave us. I hope we meet again." He shook Earl's hand and Earl left to go rescue Paula.

~~*~~

We were in my office now as we talked about how we would do our protection tonight. I told Paula that Earl had called me and was on his way, she would be safe with him. Paula asked if Earl's case was over and I said it was but I didn't know the details, Earl would fill us in on that.

Earl finally came in and we all went to the big round table in the main room. Earl spoke first, "Well I saved the day and found the girl alive, I'm just so good." He said with a big smile and gave Paula a big lip lock.

"Sure you are, but did you get paid for your work?" I asked. He had a blank look and said quietly, "Son-of-a-bitch. I didn't think about the people who hired me would be the crooks, I didn't get paid. I'll have to talk to Gaitlin to see if there's a finders fee for helping to grab the McCoys."

"Good luck with that. I'll give you the retainer he gave us to make up for it. But you still have to pay your share of the bills here." I knew Earl had money stashed away from his exploits as a black ops agent and he wouldn't starve. But I wanted to be fair.

The office door opened and in came Trapper with Becker. They came through the vestibule and I suddenly realized I hadn't seen Barry in a few days; I looked to him and asked, "Where have you been the last day or two?"

"I had to go to Lansing to re-certify for weapons training as a new detective. A day and a half of firing at cardboard criminals, but I aced it." Trapper said he did good and they sat with us.

"We got Perkins photo out to all cities and there are men around the clock watching his house. The guys at his job say they will give us a call if he shows up there, but I doubt it, he's got to know by now we have him ID'd." Trapper summarized.

Penny quietly said, "You know he's going to kill again, he's not going to let it go."

"If we could have stopped him earlier, we would have, but it takes time to track him down. He's no dummy." I said but I didn't think it would help Penny's mood.

"Captain Barrows and I talked and we decided to list him as a serial killer, using Penny's show as an excuse for the killing, whether he rationalizes his kills with people connected to the show or just goes for random people, he feels he's justified in the killings. If we don't stop him soon, there will be more deaths." Trapper said and went quiet.

Then Trapper pulled out a piece of paper from his jacket and said that he had the names and addresses of Perkin's family and a few friends, then asked me if I wanted to take a ride.

I looked to Earl and he said, "I just want to go home for the first time in a few days and get a change of clothes and show Paula my war memorabilia." He got an evil grin and Paula blushed. "But I'll be available to help when we get back." I said that works for me and stood.

Buck said he'd watch Penny like a bulldog, I told him, "Take Penny to our house, since Paula is going with Earl, may as well close up the office for the day and re-group back here in the morning. Will, shall we go do our thing?" I kissed Penny as Trapper and Becker stood, and we left.

Earl got up and went into his office, grabbed the shirt he had changed out of and then took Paula toward the door.

"Be sure you return her on one piece, Earl, or I'll be looking for you." Penny said before they could leave.

"I'll do that, my dear, all back together again safely." He grinned and they went out. Penny stood and gathered Willy's purse and put him in, then turned to Buck and said, "I'd like to do a little shopping first, you don't mind do you?"

Buck smiled and said it would be a pleasure. They closed up the office and left.

Chapter 22

Perkin's parents were very plain and quiet people reminding me of an Amish family, very humble and ordinary. Peter Perkins, the father, was a tall, strong looking man, grey hair and a grey beard that just went around his chin, no mustache. Like I said, Amish. He looked to be in his late sixties and walked with a limp. Perkin's mother was round, short and very motherly acting. Soft spoken and polite, she tried to win us over with homemade cookies. Trapper just waved off the cookies, Becker indulged himself. I said thanks but no.

"Mr. Perkins, we hate to bother you but have you talked to your son Norman recently?" Trapper asked.

"My son is dead to me, officer." He spoke quietly.

"That's Detective, and why is that sir?"

"He is an evil person, not fit to be our son. I asked him to leave two years ago and never come back. He hasn't."

"Okay how do you describe evil?"

"He would beat up on the neighborhood children and cause damage to property. The final straw came when he attempted raping a sixteen year old girl from the local school. He was nineteen at the time, old enough to go away from here."

I asked, "Why wasn't he convicted of attempted rape?"

"They had very little proof and the girl was too frightened to say it was him after he had threatened her, not publicly, but we found out that he had threatened her. We were told this by his brother David, our good son."

"Where's David now?" Trapper asked.

"He's in Grand Rapids, studying at the bible college there. We are very proud of him." Mrs. Perkins spoke up.

I thought they were the typical Midwestern family, farm bred and devout to God. But they didn't have a farm; they lived in suburbia and drove a Buick LaBaron instead of a John Deere. At least that's what was in the drive.

"I'm sorry to tell you this but we believe that Norman is our Critic killer, have you heard about it on the news?" Trapper asked.

Mrs. Perkins looked faint and dropped back in her chair. Her husband went to her and tried to comfort her. "This is what that monster has done to our family, the shame he is bringing. We will get down on our knees tonight and pray to God for all the souls of the people he had murdered."

I looked to Trapper and he just shrugged. "Mr. Perkins, I know you have lost touch with him but is there any place he may go if he can't go back to his own home? Any other family or friends he is still close with?"

"We don't know any of his heathen friends and our family wouldn't give him shelter. I'm sorry but we don't know where he could be, and don't want to know. We have no further answers for you, if you could leave now, please."

Trapper looked to me, took a sigh and stood, Becker followed suit and I got up, we thanked them and left. In the car Trapper said, "Well, at least we know he was a bad boy from early on. He hasn't changed much. I have two other people listed that he may have gone to, names I got from his co-workers at the station. He liked to talk about his exploits with his drinking buddies and did name names." Trapper started the car and we headed out.

~~*~~

Earl let Paula wander around his small apartment in St. Clair Shores, it was one of two apartments he had. The other was in Detroit and it was sparsely furnished, but he used that one as his address for when he worked for the Detroit Police force. There was a requirement that command officers and Detectives had to live in the city, but Earl wasn't fond of life there so he had his place in Detroit as a front and lived happily in the suburbs. Now that he was no longer employed by the city of Detroit, he could get rid of the extra apartment.

Paula was looking at all the pictures hanging on Earl's wall, mostly of a younger Earl in the service of the government. He was in different poses in military uniforms in different countries, probably overthrowing government regimes, she figured. He made a handsome figure in his youth, but she liked the older version just as well. Earl came out after changing clothes and was explaining the various pictures to Paula, as she listened in fascination to his tales of secrecy and undercover operations. She figured most of what he said was made up but she enjoyed his boasts.

"I'm glad you saved Margret from that animal she was married to." Paula said and kissed Earl, "I'll have to reward you for the heroics later." She gave him a coy smile and Earl laughed.

"I just do my duty and ask for no rewards, but in your case I'll accept." He kissed her back, a little harder this time when his house phone rang.

"Talk to me." He answered into phone and heard nothing at first. Then there was a small amount of breathing, Earl said, "Listen pervert, don't call here and breath heavy without talking dirty to me. It doesn't turn me on."

"Oh I don't talk dirty," came a voice on the phone, "I talk murder, and it will be murder again soon, want to know who? I'm not telling but you'll find out. Tell that partner of yours that I'm watching both of you now, Mr. Daws." Then the call went dead. Earl stood for a moment and hated being taken by surprise. He thought about calling his contacts in the bureau about back tracking the call but figured it would be useless. He did call me though.

~~*~~

"I'm sure it was Perkins, but how'd he get your home number?" I asked when Earl told me what had happened. Earl said he was listed in the book, would have been easy to find, but he didn't like the fact the Critic knew where he lived now. He said he may go stay at his Detroit apartment for a while since the location was only listed at his former police precinct and they don't give out police residence addresses to anyone.

"Well, keep me informed. We are on our way to a friend of Perkins, but I think he knows that we are on to him now. Trapper said the stake out at Perkin's home has come up with nothing. If he hasn't returned home, then he has to be hiding somewhere. I'll talk to you in the morning at the office, later." I hung up and told Trapper what Earl had said.

"Perkins is getting braver now, harassing the people he is trying to avoid, either he's crazy or very bold." Trapper offered.

"I think we know that he's crazy, but he's also bold, so he's even more dangerous. I have a feeling we will be turning up another body soon." I spoke quietly.

We arrived at the address Trapper gave me to find on my Palm TX map program. It was a boxy house on a street of similar boxy houses and all the same lawn size. Cookie cutter housing that I didn't like. We went up and rang the bell, and after a few minutes and repeatedly ringing the doorbell, the door flew open and there stood a young woman wrapped in a towel looking wet and very annoyed.

"You better not be preaching religion or I'll drop this towel and shake my boobs at you!" she yelled. Trapper brought up his badge and said, "Sorry no religion here, but can we talk to you while you hold the towel up?" She looked closer to his badge and opened the door. She said she was going to get a robe and went out of the hallway. We stood for a few minutes then Trapper was starting to look around the corner into what was the living room. We heard a noise in the back and Trapper said, "Crap," and ran towards the back of the house. The back door was open and there was a car pulling out of the drive by the garage in the alley. Trapper burst through the open door but the car was gone. He couldn't see the plates but got the make of the car.

Becker and I stood in the kitchen with the woman, now in her robe; Becker had his gun out and aimed at her. She offered no resistance. Trapper burst back through the door and yelled to the woman as he got up real close, "Was that Norman Perkins!"

She looked frightened and then quietly said it was. Trapper gave her a dirty look and got on his cell and called the local police in Madison Heights, and gave them the description of the car and explaining who was driving, but Trapper figured Perkins would drop the car and either grab another or be on foot soon.

He went to the woman and pulled her to a chair at the kitchen table and sat her down. He bent down to her and said, "Now that you are an accessory to murder, you may as well start talking, it may go easier on you."

She started to look terrified, "I don't know what you are talking about. What murder? Normy just came here to stay with me while his house was being fumigated. When you came to the door I went to get my robe and he asked who it was. I told him and he ran, that's all I know, really, honestly. I don't know anything about murder!"

Trapper stood up and looked to Becker and me. I just shrugged and said, "She may not have known."

He bent down again and asked her, "Do you know where else he may go? And don't yank my chain."

"I've heard him on the phone talking to someone named Ray, he may be going there." She replied.

Trapper looked at his list and saw the next name was a Ray Bunnert. "Was his name Ray Bunnert?" She looked to him and nodded.

Trapper pulled his cell phone and as he was pushing buttons, he explained, "We're going back to Clinton Township. We'll get him this time."

**

Chapter 23

The Madison Heights police had arrived to take the young woman in for questioning and they went over the house carefully. The Detective in charge was Tom Richmond, a friend of Trappers and he was the detective that helped me during the mistress murders. Tom came up and we shook hands and he said, "Good to see you again and on the case. Trapper needs all the help he can get." He laughed and Trapper swore.

"I don't think this woman knew about her boy toy being the killer, but doesn't hurt to talk to her. See what you can find out and let me know." Trapper asked, Richmond said he would and they took her out.

"I think Perkins has had enough time to get to his friends house and dig in. Shall we go rattle a few cages?" Trapper said and the three of us went to his car and drove back up to Clinton Township. Trapper had already called the Captain and told him the facts and needed a warrant for Bunnert's place so it would be ready when we got there. We arrived and someone from the D.A.'s office was there with the warrant. Trapper had already called for the SWAT team and extra officers, so we were ready. Everyone put on their vests, I got one from the SWAT Captain, I was definitely going to wear one after remembering the bullet I took to the chest out in New York during the strip club murders.

Everyone had arrived and was in place, Trapper and the Captain of the SWAT went to the door and banged, doing the standard warning, but no answer. The house was surrounded and if Perkins was inside he had no way out. They brought up the door ram and splintered the door then everyone charged through the opening. I could hear voices yelling clear, and dreaded that he may not be here. Then one voice yelled to get the bus, referring to the EMT unit, meaning they had a live one down.

Most of the SWAT team was coming back out now, and then Trapper appeared and said to me, "They found Ray Bunnert shot and bleeding but alive. I asked him if he was shot by Perkins, he said he was and he was able to tell me they fought about Perkins using his car and Perkins shot him. He played dead until Perkins left; we just got here about ten minutes late. Damn."

"This guy is always a few minutes ahead of us, we need to move quicker." I said.

"I got the description of the car he took and it's been put out as a BOLO, I don't think he figures we got here this fast. So we may catch him on the roads."

Trapper turned to the driveway and walked to the car that Perkins took from the woman's house and opened the door. He had on rubber gloves and handed Becker and me a pair to help look for anything that may tell us his intentions. Becker took the trunk and I took the back seat. Trapper pulled out a number of tickets from the glove box and sat sorting them out by date and place. I found nothing in the back seat so I went to Trapper to see what he was up to.

Talk Show Murders

"Tickets? Where from?" I asked.

"Mostly from out in Southfield, near where he worked for the TV station. They seem to be on the same street and all within the last two weeks, just before the killings started. I don't know if this means anything, could be the girl's tickets, but it's something to follow up on. I'll call a guy I know in Southfield P.D. to see if he can tell me anything about the area." Trapper put the tickets in a baggie and sealed it, and then he put it in the evidence box to be checked later.

"So what now?" Becker asked.

"I guess we wait until either Perkins gets caught on the road or start his crap again. I'm out of ideas." Trapper sounded tired and I wasn't feeling any more energetic. It was now just after 5:00 and I decided unless they catch Perkins in the next half hour I was going home to rest with my little family. Okay, Buck isn't little but he was like family.

Thirty minutes to the dot I told Trapper that I wanted to go back to my car, he looked around at all the excitement winding down and said he'd have Becker take me back. He would catch a ride with one of the uniforms. Becker took me to Trapper's car and we drove back talking about the events of the last few days since Becker had been out of town. He gave me the run down on his adventure shooting paper criminals and taking stupid tests to

168

make sure he was a good detective. He had aced the whole thing and was given an upgrade to detective first class.

He dropped me at my car then pulled into the motor pool at the precinct to return Trapper's car. I drove home thinking about the day and how we came so close to catching Perkins. I got to the house and parked, putting the car cover on and trudged through the new snow that fell early this morning. I should shovel the sidewalks and put down some salt on the ice that was under the damn snow. I'd do it later.

I opened the front door and saw Buck staring to the door on alert until he saw it was me. I held my hands in the air and smiled. He relaxed and sat back on the couch. Penny got up and came to me and planted a great smooch, then said they were watching my favorite show, "Castle". It was a re-run on the TiVo and I sat to watch the show featuring a crime writer following around a female police homicide detective. Penny often said she was glad Trapper didn't look like Becket, the female cop.

We watched the show as Willy came and crawled on my lap, it was relaxing to stroke the fur on his little body. He took a big sigh and slept.

The show ended and I told them about the day and how we missed Perkins by minutes twice.

Talk Show Murders

"He's going to kill again, isn't he?" Penny asked.

"I hope not but being realistic, he probably will. Trapper has no new leads, and if they don't stop him on the road, they won't catch him tonight." I said with a yawn.

"What are you yawning for; you hardly did anything today?" She laughed.

Buck spoke, "Jim gets tired just thinking."

"Hey, I have a lot of stamina for my age." I looked to Penny, "How old am I now, 59?"

"Dream on, oh wise sage. Last time I checked you were 61." She smiled.

"I heard from your station guy that they may be putting your show back on to meet his demands. Do you still remember how to interview people?" I said. She whacked my arm and stuck her tongue out.

"So what do you think about this guy?" Buck asked.

"I really don't have much to go on, his parents are anal about religion and he was a creep when he was a kid. Mom and Pop threw him out after he tried to rape a girl but was never convicted. He has a brother out in Grand Rapids attending bible school, maybe an idea to call him, see what he has to say about his brother."

We sat drinking our beer, Buck had his diet Sprite, and watched TV the rest the night. I told Buck he could use the guest room and he said that would be fine with him. We shut off the TV and went to our rooms.

Penny turned to me and said whispering, "I haven't had much good loving from you in a few days, this is unacceptable. What are you going to do about it?"

I reached over and started to pop the buttons of her silk blouse and then pulled it out of her skirt. I liked the fact that Penny always wore skirts or dresses that showed her legs, her best asset, well besides her breasts. Other than skirts she would wear the occasional shorts but never pants or jeans, that didn't bother me, I liked looking at Penny's legs. I unfastened the snap and button of her skirt and it fell to the ground. She made a little squeal of happiness and put her arms around me. I reached around her and unfastened her brassiere then pulled down the straps. She wiggled out of the bra and reached for my belt and pulled it open then proceeded to undress me. We stood in our birthday suits close. I moved her back to the bed and she sat and then pulled me down on her.

Just as we were getting hot and heavy I heard a crash; jumping up I listened and went to the door.

Talk Show Murders

Penny was swearing as I opened the door carefully and listened but heard nothing. I then heard Willy barking his head off and I smelled something that was not good. I smelled smoke. I pulled on my pants and yelled for Buck who already was out of his room and heading down the hall to the living room.

I came out to see Buck trying to smother a fire on the floor and couch with the blanket off the couch. I ran to the kitchen to grab the big fire extinguisher and came back out blasting the flames. We had the fire out in a few minutes and I saw the broken front window where the Molotov cocktail bottle had been tossed through. I went to look out and Penny came out with my Glock, I had forgotten it in the confusion. She handed it to me, Buck had his gun in his belt and we went outside to find nothing.

We went back in and Penny came to me, the damage was minor, could be repaired, but I looked to her and said, "This isn't the kind of hot I wanted tonight."

**

Chapter 24

I found a plastic tarp out in the garage and dug out the staple gun, and then Buck and I put the tarp up covering the broken glass window for the night. I'd have to call a glass company in the morning to replace the window, it was insulated glass. Perkins must have heaved the bottle hard enough to get through the window but luckily the bottle broke when it hit the window so the fire started outside the house more than inside. The snow had put out the fire on the outside, with very little damage to the exterior. We were lucky.

"I don't think Perkins would want to kill us, least of all Penny, or there would be no show. It was just his way of saying he's still dangerous." I was telling Trapper after I woke him from his sleep. "The guy is psycho, between murder and arson he has got to be stopped."

Trapper said, "I wholeheartedly agree but where do you suggest we look?"

"Maybe we need to draw him out, instead of looking for him. Give him a challenge to make him angry enough to come after us now. I have an idea."

"I hope it doesn't get some person killed." He said.

Talk Show Murders

"Yeah, that is a problem, but I'll talk to you in the morning about it, I need to talk to someone at Penny's station to see if they will go along with it. Go back to sleep and we'll talk later." I said and hung up.

Buck was sitting on the couch and he said, "I'll sleep here the rest of the night in case someone tries to get in through the window."

"That's good; just don't catch a cold sleeping too close the drafty opening." I said, and then Penny said she'd get some extra blankets for him and went to get them.

Buck was all tucked in, Penny and I went back to the bedroom and we just laid there for a while talking. "I have an idea but it may be dangerous for any number of people. Perkins could murder someone again or could go after me or even you if we do what I plan." I told her about my idea and explained a few things she would have to be ready for if the plan was to work. She said it sounded viable, and she could pull her end off, as long as it doesn't backfire.

"Yeah, that's the risk we take to catch him. We could look forever to find him; most serial killers are caught because they made a stupid mistake, which I'm hoping Perkins will do. We'll see, now I need rest and if you're not still interested in attacking my body, shall we sleep on it."

She kissed my cheek and said she had all the excitement she needed for the night. She turned and we spooned, then she was out. I just laid there thinking, I knew I wasn't going to sleep well tonight.

Morning came quickly when you only have a few hours sleep. I got up, Penny was already in the bathroom and Buck was in the kitchen making cereal. I grabbed a fruit bar and sat on the stool at the snack counter. I explained to Buck my idea and he said it sounded good to him, then my cell phone rang, caller ID said it was Earl.

"Hey super sleuth, how you feeling this morning?" He asked when I answered. I told him about our midnight attack and he swore to himself. I asked him if he could do me a favor this morning, he listened to my request.

"I'm sure Perkins is just toying with us, but it's getting to the point that I want it to stop. I have an idea I'll explain at the office. How are you two this morning?" I asked.

"We're good; Paula and I are in the office already, just waiting for you guys to show up."

I looked at my watch, it was just after 7:30 and I said, "We should be there in about an hour, if Trapper arrives, just tell him we'll be in."

"Got it. See ya then." He said and hung up.

Talk Show Murders

I did a little more thinking on my idea, would it work, would we be able to draw Perkins out to make a stupid mistake. Well, what more could we do that would be worse? I went to finish getting ready once Penny was finished in the bathroom. She kissed me on the way to the kitchen to get herself breakfast and I took a nice long shower.

By 7:10 we were ready to go. We arrived at the office and found Paula sitting at the reception desk looking wide-eyed and happy. Earl was in his office on the phone and waved when he saw us come in. Penny put Willy down and he went straight for Paula and sat up begging. She laughed and gave him a small piece of her donut. I thought we were spoiling him too much but as long as he was happy, it was good.

I went to the round table in the main room and pulled out a chair and sat. Buck went to the couch and Penny went to talk to Paula. Earl came out and spoke first, "Okay, I did what you asked me this morning, I just got off the phone with the FBI and talked to Harold Kettering, our friend from the cruise, and I asked him if they had a good profiler in the Detroit area, he gave me a number. I called him and he said he'd be more than happy to come in for your plan. He said he'd be here around nine, so we can talk before that."

"Thanks Earl, that's good. Okay, when Trapper and Becker get here I'll explain my idea." As if on cue, Trapper and Becker came through the door. "Well, that's part one of the plan, everyone is here." I smiled.

Everyone was seated and I explained that my plan was to get Perkins angry enough to want to get to one of us and hopefully do something stupid. I told Buck to be extra cautious with watching Penny and shoot to kill if need be.

"Nobody gets past me to harm Penny, count on it," he grinned.

"When the guy from the FBI gets here I'll explain the whole thing. So anyone want coffee or Pepsi?" I went to get the Pepsi from my little fridge and Penny went to make coffee. We just relaxed till the door opened and in came a rather burly, rough looking man who eyed Paula at her desk. She slid open the window and asked if she could help him. He flipped his badge and said, "Harris, FBI BAU. Is Earl Daws here?" She smiled and called Earl who was in his office getting a pad and pens. Earl came out and brought in the man and introduced all of us.

He said his name was Ben Harris from the Behavioral Analysis Unit of the Detroit branch FBI and he had a call from Harold and Earl to help us out.

Talk Show Murders

"Ben, if I can call you Ben," I said and he nodded, then I continued saying, "have a seat and I'll explain what we need."

We were all comfy and had our beverages when I looked around to everyone, "Ben, I don't know how much you know about our Critic killer, Norman Perkins?"

Harris smiled and said the Bureau was following the case, and they had asked Captain Barrows if any assistance was needed, he said maybe later.

"Good, then you know what we are up against." I told him about our exploits of the last few days and that I had a plan to draw him out. "Can you tell me what your impression is of the killer?"

"From all I have been following, he seems to be a temperate serial killer; he has a goal but not a need to kill, unless he is hiding a deeper problem, which makes him a psychopathic serial killer. He seems like a person who knows what he does and has reasons for the kill, which can make him vulnerable to errors. He doesn't seem to have long term goals for his kill, so far he has murdered three people without a plan, like indiscriminately grabbing a man off the street, so he may have a reason for this whole thing but no guidance. I think he is killing to cover some personal reason."

"He, Perkins, worked at the station that he was threatening, could he have a vendetta against the station or someone there?" I didn't look to Penny when I said that.

"Very possible, anyone here know him from the station?" He asked but was looking to Penny; he must have known who she was.

Penny sat up and said without wavering, "I didn't know him personally, just saw him around the studio, he would stand and watch the show being taped then would disappear. I never really paid much attention to him, so I can't say what he had in mind."

Trapper spoke now, "I had talked to the guys he worked with and they didn't like him much, said he was rude and opinionated. He was always complaining about the way things went in the station and he was frequently absent from his job. They did say he had problems with a few people there, nothing serious but he could get people mad at him. They didn't think there was anything too serious to make him start killing people there. His original demands were better guests on the show, which took a turn for the worse when the station took the show off the air, and then he went after random people."

"Well, he did a couple stupid things like walk in here and show himself, and then threatens Earl on the phone. Then last night he tried to burn us out of our home, but it didn't succeed very well. So far he is not very bright. Which brings me to my plan."

**

Chapter 25

Penny and I were in my office as the rest of our team sat talking at the round table. I was on the phone with Larry Lang, the studio rep and telling him what we needed to make this happen. He hemmed and hawed but said he'd talk to the owners and let them know.

"Larry, if we can't pull this off, Penny is going to option the bail out clause on her contract, so think about what you tell the owners, do you want to be the one who tells them you lost their biggest account?"

He was quiet and said he'd see what he could do. "Great, we'll be in the studio tomorrow around 10 A.M. so have all the crew and people ready to go." I said then hung up. "That should get his blood pressure up." I laughed.

Penny asked, "Do you really think it will work? I mean really?"

"Babe, I have no idea if it will or won't, unfortunately he could hide forever and keep killing people if we don't do something. People will die one way or another, but this may stop him sooner." I said hoping I was right. We went back out to the main room and announced that we now need to go to the studio tomorrow and make the arrangements for Penny's show. I said to everyone, "I explained to the studio rep about the idea and we would need plenty of promos all day today to announce the return of Penny's show tomorrow with special guests. Maybe Perkins will hold off murdering anyone until he sees the show is back on. Does everyone know what they have to do?" I asked and everyone acknowledged me. "All right, then we need to meet back here tomorrow morning at 9:00 to be to the station by 10:00. So everyone has a day off, go hide out until tomorrow."

I thanked Ben Harris and he said he'd be here in the morning, and then he left. Trapper came to me and said, "Becker and I will still be out looking for Perkins, maybe we'll find him before we need to do all this. I hope so, I don't look good on television, I know from news reports I've been on. I look terrible, like my father. Not that he looks terrible but I look old like him."

"Well, you are old." I said, he swore and then he and Becker left.

Earl and Paula were still sitting at the table and Buck was sprawled out on the couch. He asked if he could turn on the TV, I said to go ahead, but put on Penny's station to see if they are announcing her comeback. Buck took the remote and turned on the TV. Penny and I sat at the round table and I looked to Earl and said, "So you've been quiet, any thoughts?"

"I think if we piss him off enough your plan should work. We have to play it carefully so he only comes after us and not some poor slob on the street. I'll bet he's sitting in some motel room right now laughing at us. He is going to be watching the TV carefully to see if he's having any effect on us or the station, waiting for us to crumble. So if we play it right we can take him down." Earl smiled and sat back.

"We won't know till we do it. Perkins was a bit sloppy a couple of times, he's not a hardened killer, probably because he is still young. I read most serial killers are later in life not in their early twenties. He's just a punk kid with an advantage over us. Hopefully we can take advantage of his youth to get him stirred up enough the screw up."

I looked at my watch, it was just before noon and I asked, "Anyone want to go get lunch?"

Earl looked to Paula and she nodded her head, Buck said he was interested and Penny said she was starved. "I take it then everyone wants to go eat." I went to petty cash, why we had petty cash was beyond me, maybe for lunches or pizza delivery. I took out some money, Paula yelled to write down how much I took. I looked at her and just laughed. Then I stopped when she gave me a serious look. Penny said, "I train my office girls right."

I wrote down how much I took and we went out and all piled in the Crown Vic. Earl made the comment that I was taking everyone to McDonalds, I smiled and said, "I have more class than that for my friends. Only the best lunch this side of Italy."

We went to Roma Paisano, gave the car to the valet and went in. Nicky saw our little crew and came over greeting all of us, taking our group to a good table. I introduced Earl, Paula and Buck to Nicky and he smiled and said any friend of Jim and Penny is a friend of his. He signaled and had the wait staff over quickly. Everyone ordered well since it was on me, I didn't complain, but luckily I had extra money in my pocket it case. Paula told me to be sure to get a receipt for tax purposes as a business lunch.

Earl looked to her and asked, "What are you a business major?"

Penny and Paula both laughed and Paula said to him, "As a matter of fact I am. You know very little about me Earl, we always spend time in bed doing it and we have very little conversation. Well, that is going to change."

Earl got a surprised look and said, "Let' discuss it later, in private." I swear he actually blushed.

"Oh you can bet we'll talk." She smiled and kissed him. She pointed to me and said to get the receipt, I said I would.

We made small talk for a while, I had asked that we get off the subject of Perkins, everyone agreed and talked about the lousy snow and how we needed to move to Las Vegas, Penny perked up to that. Our meal came and we enjoyed the food, there was plenty for all. If you starve at Nicky's it's because you didn't finish your meal. Nicky came by frequently to check on us, being the great host he is.

"Paula, have you heard from Margret at all?" I asked as we ate.

"I called her yesterday to see how she was and tell her I was banging the guy who saved her." Everyone at the table roared but Earl, he blushed again. I was wondering if he was as tough as he says he is. "Really she is well, and happy to be away from that bastard of a husband." She looked to Earl, "That's a good reason for staying single."

I asked Earl, "You've never said if you were ever married Earl, were you?"

"God, no. I didn't have the time or interest in settling down, I was always a cop or worse, so having a wife was not in the cards."

184

"You have less stress now that you are a P.I. so do you think marriage is possible now." Penny asked pointedly, looking to Paula.

"Don't pin him on that," Paula defended, "I'm not ready to go through that again."

"Good, we have an agreement. No marriage, just great friends with benefits." He said.

"Yes, great benefits." Paula whispered in his ear but loud enough to be heard by all.

We finished our food and sat drinking our beer, pop and wine coolers while we talked. Penny was rubbing my leg, I kept pushing her off but she'd come right back. She did it again so I reached for her hand and pulled it to my crotch under the table; she jumped and gave me such a look. She smacked my hand and said to behave.

We finished and said our good-byes to Nicky and everyone left a good tip. The Valet brought my car up and we drove out onto Hayes Road. On the way to the office I asked Earl, "Are you still staying at your Detroit apartment?"

"For now, I don't trust Perkins while he is still loose. Especially after his attack on your place." I thought about that and hoped the glass company had replaced the front window at the house, I had called my brother this morning to come wait for them, he hadn't called me so I guess it went well.

Talk Show Murders

We got back to the office parking and I said, "There's not much to do here today, do you and Paula feel like coming to our house to relax?" I asked Earl.

He looked to Paula and she said it sounded good; she wanted to see our place. We went into the office to make sure everything was closed up and were just leaving when the door opened.

It was Perkins.

Earl, Buck and I dropped everything we were holding and pulled our weapons and aimed them at Perkins. He looked shocked and put his hands in the air, Earl went to the vestibule door and ordered him to come in slowly and carefully or he was going to have one hell of a headache. Perkins came in and Earl whipped him around and put his cuffs on him.

I couldn't believe it was that easy. I went to him and asked, "Why are you here, are you giving up?"

He looked to me and said, "I'm David Perkins, Norman's twin brother."

**

Chapter 26

I looked at Earl, he looked at Buck, Buck looked at me and we all looked to Perkins. Earl frisked him for weapons then pulled out his wallet and opened it, read it then showed it to me. It did say David Perkins, living in Grand Rapids. I told Earl to take off the cuffs, "I apologize for the way you were greeted but you look so much like your brother, we thought you were him. You do know the police are looking for him?"

"Yes and I can't help my appearance unless I disguise myself and that could be worse if I was stopped by the police." He replied and looked distressed.

"Were you here the other day?" Penny asked as she came forward with Paula to get a closer look.

"No this is the first time I've been here, why, did Norman come here?" David asked.

"We believe so, why are you here and how come your parents didn't tell us you were a twin?" I asked.

"My parents didn't want to associate Norman and I even though we looked alike. They even had problems looking at me because of that similarity. My parents loved me but it was a borderline thing,

I wasn't my brother but I looked like him. Something I've never been happy with."

"I can understand, but what do you want from us?" Earl asked.

"I talked to my parents last night and they told me about what Norman had done, I drove most of the night to get here to see they come to no harm. I found the card you gave my parents and came here to see if I could help." He said, and then just stood looking at the ground.

"Well, we have other plans but you can come along to watch us tomorrow when Penny goes back on the air." I said.

"Oh, is your show coming back now?" He asked looking to Penny. I didn't want to give him much information, not knowing his situation with his brother.

"Yes, it's being put back on for now. But that maybe temporary, we'll see what happens. So, we were just leaving, can you come back tomorrow morning by nine?"

He said he would and smiled then said his good-byes and left. Earl looked to me and said, "I don't trust him, for some reason, but I don't."

"Neither do I." I replied. "But we may be able to use him. We'll see. Shall we go to our place to finish the night?"

We closed up the office and drove out to our home and went in to relax. I passed out the refreshments then went into the kitchen and pulled out my phone. I called Trapper.

After he came on I explained about Perkin's twin brother and he let out a low whistle and said that was creepy. I laughed and said it was, wasn't it. Penny came into the kitchen and saw me on the phone, came over and put her arms around me from the back giving me little kisses on the neck that usually drove me crazy. I tried to ignore her while I talked but finally had to butt bump her away. She smacked the back of my head, got another beer from the fridge and went out to the other room.

"Can you get hold of Perkins' parents and get their take on the sudden appearance of brother David?" I asked, he said he would and then we finished. I went back out to our guests and said I talked to Trapper and he is going to check on David to see if he is being honest with us.

We sat and talked about things like Earl's adventures in foreign countries, but he couldn't tell us the super secret stuff because he said he'd have to kill all of us. We lasted till about eleven and then Earl said they were going. He wished us an uneventful night then he and Paula departed. Buck said he was wiped out from doing nothing all day and headed off to the guest room. Penny and I sat with Willy sleeping soundly between us. "We look like an old married couple sitting here with our dog after sending off our forty year old son living with us to bed." Penny said and laughed. I still loved to hear her laugh.

She turned her head to me and whispered, "Now that the boy is off to bed, you want to go and fool around?" I gave her a wink and said, "You betcha." I hoped we wouldn't wake Buck.

We were at the office the next morning by 8:30 and Earl with Paula had arrived shortly after. Buck had the TV set to Penny's channel and they were making a big deal about the show coming back today but this time LIVE. I had chills when I heard that but it would need to be to draw out Perkins. I hoped everyone would be able to do their parts.

FBI agent Harris arrived with two other rather big looking agents who he introduced as Hanilon and Reyburn. They were along to see that everything went smoothly if our killer showed up. I thanked them for coming. Trapper came in by himself and I took him aside.

"Anything from the parents?" I asked.

"Nope, there was no answer when I called. I sent Becker out to see if he can track them down."

"I hope he can find them, I really am a bit bugged about the sudden appearance of David." I said.

"I'll have to do a rundown on him later, if we don't catch his brother soon."

About ten minutes later, David Perkins showed up and I told him about going to the studio and gave him directions and told him to meet us there. He said he would and left.

I yelled to everyone that we needed to get to the studio. Paula was staying at the office, Earl didn't feel she was needed and didn't want her in harms way if something went wrong.

We all went out to our cars after I gave everyone directions to get there. Buck, Penny and I drove quietly to her station. I could tell she was nervous, both from going back to the show she loved doing and the thought of what might happen with Perkins.

We got to the gate and Harry was still on. He leaned out of his booth and said to me, "Jimmy, Perkins has returned, I was going to call you to tell you but here you are."

"Harry, that isn't Norman Perkins, it's his twin brother so don't go calling the cops for now, besides they're behind me with the FBI, we are protected today." I smiled and he saluted me and opened the gate after welcoming Penny back. She blew him a kiss, he grinned.

We came up to the building and parked. David Perkins came over and said he had a strange reaction from the gate guard. I said, "He thought you were Norman, expect it in the building now, most of these people know your brother."

We went in after Penny used her employee door lock card and we went to Gordy's office. He was a bit surprised to see the crowd coming into his office and asked if we could go across the hall to the conference room, we did. He called the studio rep and Lang to come down while we waited. Lang came in with a man dressed in an expensive, well-tailored suit. He was introduced as the new station lawyer and needed to clarify some points on what we needed to do, for legal reasons. I knew why I hated lawyers.

Agent Harris came over to the lawyer and badged him saying, "This is a police and FBI sting operation and comes under federal jurisdiction, so if you have any problems with our operation, take it up with the Federal Attorney's Office." He gave the guy a big sneer and the man backed off and said it was good with him. He left leaving Lang looking defenseless.

"I love intimidating lawyers." He smiled to me.

"Gordy, has Lang explained our sting to you?" I asked.

"He has and I am a little concerned about what could happen with a live broadcast." Gordy suddenly spotted David Perkins and his eyes went big. I looked to where he was staring and told him to relax. I introduced him to David and Gordy didn't shake his hand, he just stood giving him a stare. He continued, "We will have censors on the bleep button, but please warn your men not to get too rough with the language, I don't want any fines to be taken out on the station by the FCC."

"Everyone will be prompted. So, if we could go to the studio and get this set up." I led the charge and we arrived at the stage where Penny's set was all ready for her show. Make-up had set up chairs for everyone to be powdered and eye lined, but Penny went to her dressing room to have her groupies do her face.

There was no audience today as I didn't want there to be confusion if this went south on us, and so no one would get hurt. I told David that he could go sit in the seats where the audience usually sits. He went up high to the back and sat. I made note of where he was. Steve, the floor manager came in and greeted me and said he talked to Penny in her dressing room about the operation and he was all for it. He coordinated with the control booth and had the stage set up for extra chairs for the men to sit. Penny came out of her dressing room and gave me a brave smile then went to the stage. We had about twenty minutes before the show would go live, and the network was begging to pick up the feed so they could run it national. Gordy fretted about that and said they could have the tape to run later if there were no major problems. The tension was high, everyone was fidgety and then the stage lights came on to adjust. I remembered how I sat here the first time I saw Penny's show being taped and then the day when Penny was almost crushed by the light bar. I asked Buck to scout and prowl the set for anything out of the ordinary while we were getting ready. He went off to explore.

Agent Harris was to sit on the far left from Penny, followed by Trapper then Earl. I sat next to where Penny was to sit and then Steve came up and called our attention.

"Gentlemen this is going live to the people and possibly the country, they still haven't decided to let the network take the live feed. Either way, you will have to watch your language, we can be given stiff fines if the censor up in the booth doesn't bleep what you say in time even though we are on a 5 second delay, so please be careful. I know this is a hot topic, but tone it down verbiage wise. Now if you screw up on what you want to say, there is no do over. One shot to do it right. So go with the flow and cover yourself. I got no more to say but good luck. Jim it's all yours." He went to his podium to be ready for the countdown. He said to Penny that we still had about two minutes. Penny said that she remembered the live feeds we had from the magic convention and this would be a piece of cake.

I spoke now, "I'm sure everyone knows what the energy we will need to be at and what to say, so lets get this scum."

**

Chapter 27

I was looking around the studio and wondered where David Perkins was, he wasn't in his seat. I would have yelled to Buck to find him but Steve yelled "Live in ten seconds! 5.. 4.. 3.. 2.." then pointed to Penny on the silent one.

"Good afternoon people, this is a special show today, first it is live, and secondly we are going to discuss a problem facing my show and the metro Detroit area. The high jacking of our freedom by a lunatic who, as you may already know, has murdered in cold blood, four people who did no harm to anyone but live their lives. This murderer who has been identified as Norman Perkins, a former employee of this station, is terrorizing our city and we are going to discuss him today. This show is relevant to his demands in that this is a social problem, dangerous psychopathic murderers who take lives indiscriminately." She looked across the stage to me then continued, "I have as my guests today four men who represent different aspects of law enforcement. We have Agent Ben Harris from the FBI's Behavioral Analysis unit; Clinton Township Homicide Detective Lieutenant Will Trapper; Former Detroit Police Homicide Lieutenant Earl Daws, who is now a private investigator along with my husband Jim Richards, of the Richards Investigation firm. These men will talk about the murderer and what needs to be done to stop him. Now here is our show."

Penny came to the chairs as background music played and she went down the line of men starting with Harris and shook our hands. She bent down to give me a kiss. She sat in her chair and smiled to the camera. "Jim Richards, as most of you know is my husband and has gotten a bit of notoriety himself for numerous crimes he has solved starting from the famous Classmate Murders recently portrayed in a TV mini-series to the breaking up a slave trade ring in New York. His experience with serial killers is well known."

I thought she was building me up a bit too much but what the heck. I smiled at her as she said, "I'll turn this over to you Jim."

"First to discuss crimes of serial murderers, I have invited Agent Ben Harris of the FBI's Behavioral Analysis Unit. For those unfamiliar with the BAU, if you have seen "Criminal Minds" on television you'll know what he does, he's a profiler." I turned to Ben and said, "Ben give us a rundown on your opinion of Norman Perkins."

Ben smiled and told the viewers about serial killers and their nature. He talked of famous serial killers from history to give credence to Perkins. "As I have been observing Norman Perkins, he is not your typical serial killer, he doesn't have a well thought out plan; he is just hitting at random victims and voicing threats. A real serial killer just murders and rarely asks for attention." He went on a bit more about Norman's psychology and his desire to get revenge on his supposed enemy.

Ben looked to me, I said, "As Penny has said, this show is live, we are doing this to allow Norman Perkins to answer to his demands and give him a chance to explain his reasons for what he is trying to accomplish or if he even knows what he is doing, at least explain it to us Norman." I said looking directly to the camera. "There should be a number in front of me that Norman can call if he has the guts and talk to us." I could see the number in the monitor in front of me. "And to you people watching, please don't tie up our phone lines with useless questions or comments, let's give this coward a chance to talk."

I turned to Trapper and said, "Detective Trapper, you have presided over a number of serial cases including the one we shared with the Classmate murders. What is your take on this?"

Talk Show Murders

Trapper cleared his throat and took a drink from the water glass that the studio had set out for us. "This killer is just a disorganized lunatic, and he has some motive for killing other than wanting to see better subjects on this show. He's hiding his cowardice behind a social platform for whatever his problem is. But we don't know what it is because he won't come forward to explain his motive. He is a coward and should just get on with explaining his purpose and stop <<BLEEP>> around."

I tried not to laugh when he said it, but I'm sure they caught it up in the booth.

Trapper apologized and went on describing how Perkins had murdered his victims, being a bit graphic but getting the point across. I saw Steve at his podium on the phone and he smiled to me. He gave Penny the signal for commercial break and they went out to break. Steve came over and said the phone line was lit up with people wasting time, all the lunatics in the area were wanting their say. I thought about it and asked if we could take a couple of those calls to help draw him out. Steve said he'd get to the control room and let them know. Steve gave the count down again and Penny continued.

"If you are just joining us, we are discussing the murderers of people by our so called serial killer, Norman Perkins. Jim Richards will now have us hear what a few callers have to say. These calls have been screened by our staff so please don't call to give your opinion on the economy. Jim." She said to me and I said, "Is the caller there?"

"Yes, I have been a faithful watcher of Penny's show since it came on five years ago. This is tragic that this person has to use the show for his personal vendetta, he has to be crazy."

I cut her off by saying, "Thank you for your comments, we have another caller?"

"Yeah, I'm Mike from Clinton Township and I want to say this guy should have his <<BLEEP>> removed. He has no sense of what he does, and he is ruining this good country."

I cut him too. "All right, thanks, now I'd like to get Earl Daws' opinion of this. Earl has been a cop for over twenty years and before that he worked in the CIA. He has the super-agent talents that we need to stop this killer. Earl, what's your take?"

"Jim, I have dealt with killers worse than this amateur, he is bush league compared to Manson, Gein, Bundy, Dahmer or Gacy. They were real serial killers; they had a purpose or madness in their crimes. Not this putz who is trying to do what he can't handle."

I sat listening to what everyone was saying. They may not be accurate in their descriptions of serial killers but they were coached to make Perkins mad and do something stupid. Then it came. Steve waved to me and held up a dry marker board, with the words, "Perkins on phone!!"

I interrupted Earl and said, "We have a special guest on our phone, Norman Perkins is going to speak to us. Norman are you there?"

"Yeah I'm here you <<BLEEP>>. You people don't know squat about what I do. You all judge me and treat me like crap, like all the <<BLEEP>> people at that stinking station. I hate them all!"

While Perkins was talking I could see agents Hanilon and Reyburn talking on their radios. The idea was to get Perkins to call in to hopefully spew about what he had done and we could get a phone fix on him. Trapper had all his buddies on alert in their cities to go after Perkins once they had a fix on him. Now if we could keep him talking.

"Do you know what it is like to be the bad son, eh, Richards? My parents treated me like crap, they did! That's all right because I finally dealt with them this morning, you'll find their bodies all nicely sitting in their chairs in their living rooms watching your show, but they won't see it will they!? They didn't want me so I don't need them! I'll deal with my brother later, when I can get to him. Oh you can try to protect him but I'll get him!"

I had to keep him talking, "Norman, you murdered people for what? You had no purpose but hating people who treated you badly, why Norman?"

"That fruit Parker came in all bouncing around like a <<BLEEP>> star. I accidentally walked into him in the hall and he treated me like dirt, like a fly to be smashed! I took care of him, and then I made a plan, to get back at the people who treated me like crap. He deserved it!"

"What about the recycling guy?" I asked.

Perkins laughed, "I did that, I set him up as a guest, it was a suggestion to Joy in scheduling, she like it so asked him on the show. He was a deacon at a church I used to be forced to attend by my <<BLEEP>> parents into going; the son-of-a-bitch molested me when we were alone in the church basement. The bastard deserved to die!!"

I was feeling chills listening to his rant. Penny was holding my hand now and I could feel her squeeze it when he talked about killing.

"And Morty, the lawyer? What did he do to you?"

"Oh, yeah, that pig. He would come into the station and always request me to do his bidding and carry his papers around, he would sit in his tiny office and gloat about how he was better than me and I would always be just a mail boy. I hated him too."

Talk Show Murders

Hanilon was waving to us and I knew he must have a fix on him. I didn't want to cut away to commercial while we had him on the line. I turned to Earl and said quietly, to keep him talking. I excused myself and went off the stage. I went to Hanilon and asked what he had. He said that Perkins was calling from a cell phone but the call was being redirected through his home phone, they were trying to track the call but it may not work in the time we had. I was disappointed. I went back to the stage and sat for a minute. Perkins was quiet now.

"Norm, you are a coward. We won't give you a platform any longer, why don't you just turn yourself in or better yet take your own useless life. Steve cut this coward off." I said to him and he gave me a strange look then called the booth to cut the call.

"I'm sorry people but we don't need to listen to his drivel, he is useless and will be a nothing the rest of his useless life. So Norm if you are still watching, go to <<BLEEP>>"

**

Chapter 28

The show was close to winding down so Penny thanked us for making this an event to remember. They went to extra commercials since they didn't cut away when Norman was on the line. Gordy came down from the booth and asked me what happened at the end.

"The Feds couldn't get a fix on his location so we had no where to go. I just said what I did to piss him off, he wanted to kill people who dissed him, well I dissed him in front of the viewers, so maybe he'll try to come after me now."

Trapper and Earl were standing next to me and Earl said he figured that's what I was doing, so we would have to be on the look out for Perkins to stage an attack.

"Speaking of Perkins, where did David Perkins go to, he was in the audience seating?" I asked as Penny came up and said she was going to close the show and go to her dressing room. She went to the stage and gave a brief summary and said good-bye. I thought she meant it when she said it, at least it sounded like a final good-bye. I hoped she wasn't giving up.

Buck came up and I said to everyone to go look for our missing twin. Buck, Earl and Trapper went off and I thanked Harris for his help. He said it was too bad they couldn't get his location, but they'd still be glad to help with whatever we needed. I said it would be a great help. He went off with his two sidekicks and out the door from the studio. I stood alone and watched Penny go into the hall to her dressing room. I was standing there when I saw Becker run into the studio, out of breath. I yelled to him and he came over. Trapper came around a corner of a set and saw Becker heading towards me and came over.

"Barry what's the matter?" I asked.

"I tried to call but everyone's phone was off." I said because we were on the show, he continued, "I went out to Perkins' parent's house and found them dead." He said breathing hard.

"We already know this; Perkins confessed it over the phone to us." Trapper told Becker.

"Yes, but there's more. While the local police was there processing the crime scene after I called them, one of the neighbors came over to see what was going on. He said he was shocked to hear they were murdered. He knew them for years. I asked about David, their other son and he said David was in college out in Grand Rapids, I said I knew that. Then the man said the younger son probably did this, he was a bad one. I asked him what he meant by younger; he said that Norman was the younger of the two brothers. I said he was a twin wasn't he?

The man laughed and said David and Norman were about five years apart, hardly twins."

"Crap I thought he was not right, damn it, he was Norman! I don't believe it, we had him right here all this time." I yelled. Trapper got on his phone and called Harris back saying Norman was in the studio. I went on, "Norman must have gone off somewhere and called on his cell phone to his house number and got it redirected to here. He was talking to us from this station!"

I paused to think, then continued, "Okay, he may not know that we know he is not David, hopefully he will come back to us." Earl and Buck came up and I filled them in on Perkins. They said they couldn't find him anywhere nearby, they looked but they hadn't covered the whole studio, just the immediate vicinity. Harris and his men came back and we filled them in. We stood waiting but I said, "This is silly, he needs to be found, unless he has left the studio. Buck go see if his car is still here, you remember it don't you?" He said he knew his car and went to check. "Everyone turn your phones back on if you haven't."

Gordy came over and said, "The station is being flooded with calls, the majority says it was great, we had a few prudes say it was disgusting. But the network watched the feed and wants to run it with a side show explaining what our show was about. I told Gordy quietly that David Perkins was actually Norman. "I knew it, he just didn't seem right to me. I had come across Norman too many times to be fooled by him. The little prick."

"Well, let's go find him. This time we search the whole studio. Trapper, call your buddy here in Southfield and have them surround the studio and send some men in to help search." Trapper got on his phone and called.

We started to go search when my cell phone rang. The Caller ID said it was Penny. I answered and suddenly felt my nerves tighten, it was Perkins. I covered the phone and yelled for Earl, who was closest, he came back.

"You better not be telling me you have Penny you asshole." I yelled into the phone.

"Oh, Jimmy baby you can dish it out but can't take it. I don't want your precious wife, I want you. You insulted me and I want my revenge, maybe taking the one thing you really love will make you suffer."

"Perkins, don't harm her, I'll trade myself for her, don't take it out on her, please." I toned my voice down so he wouldn't get too excited. I covered the mouthpiece of my phone again and said, "He has Penny, he has to still be in the studio. Get everyone out who doesn't need to be here and get a fucking army in here now!" Earl went off to get the rest of the guys.

Bob Moats

I went back to the phone and asked if he would trade, he said he'd think on it and hung up. "Damn, damn!"

Gordy came by again and said he was told to get everyone out of the studio, why? I told him Perkins took Penny and we need to empty the studio so we can get him without endangering anyone else. Gordy agreed and went off to start the evacuation. Trapper came up and said that the Southfield police were posted outside and I said to have them watch the doors and give them copies of his picture. I knew he wouldn't try to drag Penny out of the studio so he'd have to lay low inside.

About twenty minutes later the station was empty except for the few people in the control rooms, but they could lock themselves in. The station had to go on even though most of the programming was on automatic.

I took Earl with me to Penny's dressing room and we found Celeste, the head of make-up, sitting with Willy. I asked if she saw Penny, she said she hadn't. I went to her and said quietly, "Take care of Willy for us and get out of the studio, go wait in your car till you hear it's safe." She asked why? I said, "Norman is in the studio and he has Penny." Celeste looked shocked and I asked Buck to walk her out of the station. He took her out and down the hall to the employee entrance. He opened the door and was met by three Southfield police, who were ready to jump Buck. Celeste yelled that he was a good guy so they relaxed and Buck asked them to escort her to her car. One of the officers did.

Buck came back and we started to search the place from front to back. It was annoying that I had already done this once before when I was searching for Penny during the Classmate murders. I knew the frustration of all the places one could hide in this building. Buck was trying to give me words of encouragement but I was focused on the search. I stopped and had a thought. I pulled my cell phone and dialed Penny's cell. I listened to it ring then I heard it click on. "I was wondering when you were going to finally call." Came the voice.

"Have you thought about an exchange?" I asked quietly.

"I'm mulling it over; I may be prone to agreement. But you'd have to do some real begging when I get you." He hung up again. I looked at the phone and redialed. He came back on, "What do you want now?"

"Tell me where we can make the trade, I'll do it."

"Oh, you'll have to find me to make the trade. I want to make you suffer a bit more."

I wanted to kill him, but I didn't say it. "Well, give me a hint." I hoped his ego would give him away.

"Oh, it's deja vu for you." Then he hung up again. I looked to Buck and thought hard on what he meant.

Buck asked what he said, I told him, "Doesn't that mean you've been there before?" He said.

I was ready to kiss Buck but didn't. I knew where they were now. I started that way from memory of being there before during the Classmate Murders. It was in the back storage area where the psychos Davey and Julia took Penny. It had to be. Buck and I got to the door and I told Buck to go through the store room that came around into the main storage room, the same way he went when he whacked Julia on the head. He went through door and I went in the entrance to the prop storage room. It had changed a bit, new sets and props were stored and I came around a set flat and saw her, Penny. She was tied to a chair now, the bed from before was gone. Her mouth was taped then she saw me, starting to shake her head. I looked around and didn't see Norman, so I went to Penny, she was still shaking her head. I stood in front of her and tried to get her loose when I felt the bash to my head. I went down.

**

Chapter 29

I was on the ground looking up at the overhead lights, my mind was swirling. I hadn't been knocked out completely I guess, since I could see Perkins hovering over me and Penny was still tied to the chair. I was wondering where Buck was, he needed to make his grand entrance now to save the day, but I didn't see him. Perkins was bending over me gloating and saying something but my ears were still ringing from the blow to the head so he sounded muffled.

Suddenly, I could hear a crashing noise to my left and Perkins stood up holding a gun out at the noise. He fired once and then turned to go towards where the entrance was. He ran just as I heard another gunshot but this one didn't come from Perkins, it had to be Buck finally. My sense of time was a bit distorted; Buck must have come in quicker than I thought.

Perkins was out of my line of sight as I still lay on the ground looking at all the pretty stars. Suddenly in the middle of all those stars I saw Buck's bright round face like a Greek God looking down upon me. His bald head gleaming in the overhead lights and he was giving me his trademark smile. I was able to say, "Go get the bastard; I'll be fine in a minute." Did I say that? Buck was hesitating, I said again, a little louder this time, "Go get him! I'll be fine." Buck nodded and went off in Perkins' direction.

I turned my head and saw my Penny still tied to the chair; I mustered up my strength and sat up. The world started spinning again and I closed my eyes to make it stop. I peeked out and the room was slowing down, then I got to my knees and walked on them towards Penny. She was mumbling something, but I still couldn't hear too well. I pulled out my knife and cut the duct tape that held her wrists together. She brought her hands up and yanked the duct tape off her mouth, then yelled at me, "Were you trying to get yourself killed!? First rule of being a P.I. is watch your back!"

She was alright, I smiled and she helped me to stand. My head was still hurting and I reached to the back of it to see if there was any blood, there wasn't. I took Penny to the entrance door, this time with my Glock out, tried the doorknob and opened the door cautiously. I peeked out and didn't see anything so we went out. I thought I saw Becker down the long hallway, I called to him. He came running up and said he was glad to see Penny was safe.

"Barry, get your gun out now. Perkins is in the area somewhere being chased by Buck. He has a gun, must have brought it with him. Take Penny out of the building and get her safely with the Southfield police, do it now, Barry." I kissed Penny and told her to get moving, she knew the most direct way out of the building so she led Becker out.

I leaned against the wall to steady myself after she had gotten out of sight, I wanted her to think I was better now, but I was still watching the room go in a different direction than my head. I stood for a few moments when I heard a couple of gun shots from somewhere in the studio to my right. I hoped they got him.

I was starting to feel a little better, so I stood up straight and the earth was not moving as fast now. I went in the direction that I thought I heard the gun fire from and ran into Earl as I went through the hallway door.

"Jim are you all right? I saw Buck and he said you were down." He said in a hurry.

"I'm fine, anything on Perkins?"

"He's still in the building; we got most of the Southfield police combing the studio for him. Buck was on his tail but he said he lost him." There were a couple more gun shots from another direction and we ran that way.

We came into a studio where it looked like they did a cooking show and it was quiet. We went through into the next room, which looked to be another storage room like the one I got hit in. I thought that Perkins could hide in this place for years before we would find him. We came out to the hallway where the offices were, Gordy's office was just down the hall and the mail room was that way. Earl and I went towards that end, I looked into the mail room hoping Perkins would be there sorting mail but it was empty.

More gun fire, a few more shots this time. Did they have him cornered? I could only hope. We went that direction, although the gun fire seemed to be coming from all around us now, Perkins must be moving fast. I was a bit worried that someone would get hurt in the crossfire; I asked Earl, "Did they get everyone out safely?"

"Yeah, once the word got out, there were people streaming for the exits like salmon going upstream to mate." I smiled at his reference then we went through another hallway door into the lobby. I looked out at Ten Mile Road with all the cars and trucks busily whizzing by, going about their business, not caring about the drama that was going on just feet away. The hallway door we had just come through suddenly burst open and Trapper came through. He smiled at us and asked if we had seen Perkins?

"Not coming this way, he's still lost in the studio."

"Well, the building is surrounded and there are cops and now SWAT has arrived, so his ass is meat if they find him." He went back into the hall as I went to sit on a couch in the lobby. Earl came and stood by. "Don't want to get in on the fun?" He asked.

"There's enough law enforcement in and around the place, I'd just end up shooting myself in the confusion." I sighed and sat back. He came to sit next to me.

"You know, you do really attracted crime like Penny said. You're a murder magnet." He chuckled.

"Isn't that what you and Harold said about me when we were in Tahiti, you two said I had the 'death eye', I attracted murders."

"Ah, yes, the old death eye, it is a fact you know. First discovered in 1792, when a young investigator for Pinkertons tracked down a murderer and they saw he had the death eye." Earl grinned to himself.

"You're making this all up aren't you? You are such a bull artist; I never know when to believe you." I grinned back to him.

"Still thinking about Vegas?" He asked after a few moments of silence.

"Yea, it's looking better all the time." I said as another gun shot was heard but this time closer to our location. We got up quickly and were just going through the lobby door when it burst open and

Bob Moats

Perkins ran between us going full steam. It took Earl and me a second to get our bearings to realize it was him. We turned drawing our weapons just as he hit the front door to the road. I was wondering where the Southfield cops were, they weren't outside the doors. Probably were called inside to find Perkins. The Lobby doors flew open again and out poured Buck being followed by Trapper and a number of Southfield cops. I pointed the way to the door and they went that way. Earl and I followed.

We went out to see Perkins standing at the curb of the busy road. We were afraid to shoot because of the traffic and the businesses across the road. The cops all ran towards Perkins, he had a look of panic on his face and turned to the road and ran across.

He never made it all the way. As soon as he was in the second lane over, a five ton service truck was bearing down on him and he froze in front of it. We saw him go into the grillwork of the truck then disappear under it. The driver was pushing hard on his air brakes and finally stopped just down a bit from where Perkins got hit. All the cops and my crew ran out as the Southfield cops were stopping traffic now. We went to the truck as the driver was having fits about the incident. Perkins wasn't at the front of the truck now, but one officer yelled that he was in the back. We went around and saw him lying under the back axle; he was pretty much smashed up.

Talk Show Murders

Trapper smiled, turned to us and said that the Southfield police can take it from here so he, Earl, Buck and I all went back to the building. We weren't needed anymore.

About an hour later, everyone was back at their jobs in the station and Penny was sitting in her dressing room with Willy on her lap. Trapper was talking to a Lieutenant from Southfield that he knew, and they were discussing the incident. Earl was on the phone to Paula back in the office telling her about it all. I sat on the couch in the dressing room still nursing my head, holding a cold wet face cloth on it.

Buck came in and sat next to me and said, "They scraped Perkins up and took him off in the meat wagon. He was pretty much dead as soon as the truck hit him, the coroner said. I guess he wasn't as smart as we thought he was."

Penny looked to me, her eyes were a bit red from crying I supposed. She came over with Willy and sat next to me and whispered in my ear, "Can we move to Vegas now?"

**

Chapter 30

Penny and I stood at the fountain of the Bellagio Hotel watching the streams of water shooting up hundreds of feet in the air and making its synchronized dance around the huge reflecting pool. I was sitting on the marble wall that separated the sidewalk from the water and Penny was standing next to me holding tightly to Willy. I looked down the way and saw Deacon and Lynn watching the water also. They had seen it hundreds of times but it was still fascinating to watch.

We had been back in Las Vegas now for two days and we were getting our lives back in sync. Penny had decided to option her bail out clause on the show since she had enough money squirreled away to live well for a good number of years. She wanted to enjoy life now and as much as she'd miss her show and all the people who she worked with, it was time to move on.

Deacon had been a good friend since we first met when he was assigned to protect Penny during the Classmate Murders and he met Lynn, a Vegas homicide detective, when we were first out here for Penny's television promotion. Deacon decided to stay in Vegas with Lynn since they had started a budding romance. The big guy said he was happy living here and he said he loved Lynn more every day.

The weather was warm, in the nineties, which was normal for winter in Vegas during the day. I knew that it had snowed in the city only a couple times in the last ten years; mostly the snow stayed high up on the mountains that surrounded Sin City. That was as close to snow as I ever wanted to get ever again.

I could see that Penny was relieved and happy since we came out here. We still hadn't committed to the move but we were about a month away from it. We would still keep the house for a place to stay when we were back in Michigan; Earl could watch the office and we could still go back for short visits during the summer months to see family and maybe take a case of spousal spying. But no more murders.

Deacon and Lynn came down the sidewalk to us and Deacon asked when was the big day. I looked at him, and asked what big day?

"When you get smart and make the move." He laughed, "We've been figuring it had to be someday, time's wasting away and you're not getting any younger. I have a friend in real estate who is listing a great house just outside the city on the way to Mt. Charleston. It has a great view of the skyline and the valley. I can have him show you guys the place." He sounded like a little kid asking if the new kids on the block would come and play with him.

Lynn gave him a kiss and patted his shoulder, "Let them decide what they want to do before you start making plans for their future."

Penny smiled and said, "Deacon, you can tell your friend that we want to see the house. At least to look." She turned to me and gave me her evil little smile.

Buck and Maria came running across the road, something you are not supposed to do in the city, they had crossovers for that. Too many pedestrians were killed or injured on the streets here. Then I thought about Perkins and how I had watched him go into that truck, something I wouldn't soon forget. I'd try to put it out of my mind though.

"Maria won two hundred dollars on slots over at the Tropicana just now." They both were smiling like idiots, but happy idiots.

"Good, then you can buy us lunch." Deacon said and laughed. Maria smiled at her big brother and said it would be her pleasure, but it had to be a buffet, it's cheaper.

We all went to the MGM Grand across the way and into the restaurant that had a good buffet. We filled our plates and went to sit and eat our food. I was hearing the sound of the slot machines in the background making that ting, ting, ting sound then the melody it played as the wheels spun and hopefully hit for some lucky person.

I was taking in the atmosphere and loving it. Penny was feeding Willy in his purse and I presumed the restaurant frowned on dogs at the tables, but the purse hid him well enough and he was tiny enough to not be noticed so easily.

We finished and went to Deacon and Lynn's apartment. We sat around talking, drinking our refreshments and eating snacks. I was having my beer since I wasn't driving; I had Buck drive the rental car. He was staying at Maria's, as always and would drop Penny and me at Caesar's Palace where we were staying this trip out.

My cell phone rang and I saw it was Earl, "Hello, I'm out right now but leave a message," I joked. He said, "Hey, I got a case from a sexy woman who thinks her husband is trying to kill her, you interested in helping?" I said you have the wrong number and hung up. I was suppressing a good laugh and Penny asked me who it was, I said those damn telemarketers.

I saw Deacon stand and motion to me to follow him. I kissed Penny and said the boys are going to go talk. I went over to the balcony that came out from their apartment over looking the mountains that I loved to admire. Deacon could see me taking in the sight.

"You know that house has a great view of the Vegas Skyline and mountains." He said quietly.

"I'm sure it does and if you get Penny to see it, we'll have place to live."

"What's in your future, Jim?" He asked as we were silent for a moment.

I turned to him and said, "You remember Shadow, Penny's cat?"

"Of course, the cat who loved to attack you every chance he got." Deacon smiled at the memory of the cat attacking my leg on the first day in Penny's house.

"Well, he slipped out one day, like he often did but this time he didn't come back. He had gone out before and was only gone for a few days. But this time he was gone over a week. Penny was upset, but she had Willy to fill the void. One day when Penny was at her studio, I was home cutting the grass. Yes, I do yard work, before you make a snide comment. I was cutting up by the road when I spotted a dark lump in the drainage ditch just off the shoulder of the road. I went to see and it was the body of Shadow. He must have tried to cross the road and got hit. I buried him in the back by the lake and told Penny about it when she got home. For closure. She got over it eventually but then last week when I watched Perkins get hit by that truck, Shadow flashed into my mind for a second. The road is always there before us, we can sit on the curb and watch the traffic go by or we can wait till the traffic is clear and cross. Or some people just lunge out into the traffic and do a dance to avoid getting hit. Like that Frogger game we used to play. I realize life can be short and Penny has been subjected to death a number of times, more than I like. I think it's time to cross that road, but looking both ways."

We stood watching the sun go down on the valley, the bright red sky now getting ready for the lights of the city to illuminate the night sky. I turned back to the apartment and saw Penny sitting and laughing at some joke someone told, I looked to Deacon and said, "It's time for a change, my friend, time for a change."

**

THE END

For every ending there's a new beginning.

~~*~~

Preview of the eleventh Jim Richards book, "Sin City Murders"

Bob Moats

Chapter 1

The woman stood at the edge of the Stratosphere tower looking out over the Las Vegas valley. From her vantage point she had a real nice view of the city, and all its people moving around like ants. Of course being almost a thousand feet in the air helped to make the people look like ants and right now the woman could care less about all those people. At that moment she was more concerned about how she would look after she hit the ground below. Maybe this wasn't the best way to kill one's self. She thought about going back in the building and maybe buying some rat poison and do herself in that way. But what if she didn't take the right amount? She'd end up getting her stomach pumped and being put away for observation to see if she was stable enough to be let loose again. She hated the institution she had just gotten out of; she had been there because she had tried to slit her wrists, which she botched.

Okay, jumping off the tallest structure west of the Mississippi was something that even she couldn't botch on her own, so this was the way to do it. She looked down, something she shouldn't have done, but took a huge breath and did a beautiful Swan dive out from the footing. Her body floated downward being pummeled around a bit by the high winds that came across the valley every so often to make life miserable for the city. She was now floating over towards the busy Las Vegas Boulevard below instead of the parking lot she had hoped to hit. As she watched the ground below coming up in seemingly slow motion, she wondered what points of her life would flash before her eyes; she wanted to re-live a few things that she had enjoyed in her miserable life.

Her body was now directly over the busy boulevard of tourist cars going on their way to gamble or watch an expensive show. She didn't care, she just wanted to die. By the time she had made impact, a household furniture moving truck had pulled up below her and she crashed through the top of the cargo portion into a pile of mattresses that barely cushioned her fall. She was not in good shape, but she also wasn't dead, she lay there hurting badly and just mumbled, "Crap!"

~~*~~

Penny had already started to plan decorating the home we purchased just outside the city of Las Vegas. The home had this fantastic view of the entire Vegas strip, all it's casinos and hotels standing tall, and the mountains looming up behind the strip. We were almost on the foot of the mountains behind us; we had a good sized backyard but since it started to go upwards to the high cliffs behind us, we had no great view back there, but it was private. The wall of rock also provided a natural fence so we couldn't be attacked by pirates from the rear, unless they rappelled down the face of the mountain. Willy was loving the large area to run, it was peaceful and fairly secluded. The next neighbor to us was about a city block away on the long, winding road that led over to Mt. Charleston. We were a bit out of the way from the city, but it would be nice because of the seclusion.

Our good friends, and a couple of Las Vegas Metro Police's finest detectives, Deacon and Lynn had been busy helping us take stuff from the moving truck into the house. I had paid my son to drive the moving truck out from Michigan, with my Crown Vic being towed behind and he help with unloading the truck also. He saved me from having to strain my back.

Penny and I had driven back out to Vegas in the Lincoln limo and the trip took us just four days of travel which was nice being in the comfortable car. We had gone back to Michigan to sort our lives and bring back with us just what we needed. Penny and I decided to let my son, his wife and our grandson move into the Michigan house while we were out in Vegas, until next summer when we would go back to stay a couple weeks with the family for a visit. My daughter-in-law and grandson were presently staying in the house until my son went back, so the house wasn't unattended. After we had emptied the moving truck, we took it to the nearest U-Haul rental place to drop off, then we drove my son to the airport and he flew back, being picked up at Metro Airport in Detroit by my brother.

Talk Show Murders

Buck had decided since everyone was deserting him, and with coaxing from Maria, he would also move, but keeping his house and options open for going back. He had his brother help him pack a small moving truck and towed his classic T-Bird in back. He wanted the car with him in Vegas to be able to really enjoy his "ride".

Penny and Lynn had made a number of shopping trips to the huge mall not far from us, another factor in Penny's decision that we buy the house. They made a number of trips in Deacon's big Chevy truck and then I was finally asked to go with Penny to pick out some furniture. We found a nice store on Lynn's recommendation and bought a houseful of furniture, to be delivered in the next two days or it would be free. I'd like to see them make good on that promise, the furniture cost a fortune.

The house was now taking on a little shape, Penny had bought curtains and we spent a couple hours putting them up. Deacon was handy since he was taller than all of us, so he had the job of putting up the hardware for the curtains. We manage to cover the front of the house to keep prying eyes out, but I doubted there would be many eyes out here. Penny was like me when it came to windows being uncovered at night, we liked the curtains closed.

It was just before night fall and we all sat in the front yard watching the sun's light slowly move down the mountains across from us. The lights of Vegas were just coming on in full force and it was a beauty to behold. The beam of light from the Luxor had been turned on and I remembered our first trip out here when I was shot and I hallucinated that I sat on the top of the pyramid.

"So without bedroom furniture, where you two going to sleep tonight?" Deacon asked as he laid back on the chaise lounge Penny and Lynn had dragged home from Wal-Marts along with the rest of the lawn chairs they could get in the truck.

"We're camping out. I had our gear thrown in the moving truck from Michigan and we are pitching the tent and rolling out the sleeping bag." I replied as Penny smiled next to me. "The camping stuff will come in handy as we plan on camping a lot up on Mt. Charleston."

"It's going to be cold tonight." Deacon warned, "It's still winter here you know, and at night the temperature can drop in the low thirties."

"We're camping in the living room, so we'll be warm and toasty with a roaring fire in the fireplace." I answered.

Lynn's cell phone rang and she answered, listened for a minute then hung up smiling widely. "Want to hear something really different?"

Talk Show Murders

We all waited for her to speak, "It seems a woman took a nose dive off the Stratosphere and landed in a truckload of mattresses. She lived and she's mostly stunned, she's lucky. The big deal was she left a suicide note saying she was killing herself because she couldn't bear the shame of a murder she thinks she committed. She's not in shape to explain tonight so I've been assigned to go talk to her if she comes around tomorrow."

Penny looked to me and mumbled, "Murder rears its ugly head again, don't even think about going near her or you'll sleep out with the rocks."

I laughed and said I'd stay away. I looked down the road and could see Buck coming up in his T-Bird with Maria, and after they parked the two of them came over to us with a magnum of champagne. "A little house warming gift." He grinned. I thanked him and said we didn't have any glasses yet. Penny said to hold on and went into the house coming back out with a box of glassware she had bought earlier today on one of her shopping trips with Lynn. She opened the box and handed me the first glass after I popped the cork off the bottle. I poured the liquid and handed them out to everyone. Buck had his small bottle of Sprite and we toasted.

"To good friends, good house, good weather, good life, good night," and I drank.

After it was finally dark and the lights of Las Vegas were brilliant on the floor of the valley, along with the beam of light shooting up from the Luxor Pyramid, everyone was tiring so they all left. Penny went into the house and brought a couple more beers from the fridge and we sat relaxing, listening to the night air blowing around the hills. It was a more gentle breeze now, better than the howling winds earlier. We held hands as we sat watching the circus of Sin City moving and glittering before us.

"Why didn't we do this a year ago?" Penny asked.

"I don't think we were ready for it. You had to finally decide to get away from your show and I had to get away from my family. It was the right time now and I'm not regretting it at all."

She suddenly stood and kissed me on the top of my bald head. "I'm getting a bit chilly. I think I'll go in and start a fire, care to join me? You can pitch the tent and we can cuddle." She gave me her evil little smile and said, "Then we can christen the house."

She went off into the house with Willy following her, I sat for a moment longer just feeling the atmosphere of the place, I was home now.

**

CONTINUED IN BOOK...

229

Talk Show Murders

~~*~~

Jim Richards Family of Readers

Thanks to the following people who are now part of the Jim Richards Family of Readers. They have read a book or more and enjoyed them. They all volunteered to be included in the list. If you are a fan of the books, send me your full name and you will be included in future books. Send your name to murdernovels@bobmoats.com to be added here and on the website.

* Achim Feifel * Al Norris * Alex Wheatley * Alexandra Delporte-Wilkinson * Amy Tapia * Andrea Bryan * Anne Shepherd * Arianda Sugar * Arlene Markowski * Ashley Augustus * Audra Hall * Barbara Hughes * Barbara Sammons * Barbara Schuler * Barbara Zirger * Beth Donohue Plenskofski * Betsy Childress * Beth Gibson * Bill Sandy * Bill Tornquist * Billie-jo Collie * Boni J Rychener * Carl Bishopric * Carla Lewis * Carole Henderson * Carolyn Conroy * Carolyn Riddle-Linington * Cassy Bailey * Cathie Turner * Chad Hudson * Charlotte L Duran * Cheryl L. Everett * Cindy Ackley Nunn * Cindy Valstad * Connie Bancroft * Corinne Kay O'Daniel * Dana Robbins Chuchran * Dana Wichita * Danielle Monique * Darren Heald * Dave Travers * David Wilkinson * DeAnn Jannereth * Deanna Miller * Deb Breuker Balbo * Debbie Carter * Debbie White * Deborah Fartuch * Deborah Gauze * Deborah Sullivan * Dee King

Bob Moats

* Denise Freeman * Diana Carver * Dixie Beck * Donna Gould * Donna Thompson * Donny Minter * Doris Kight * Eddie Moore * Eric Walters * Felicia Annette Bradfield * Francine Menor * Gail Chesney * Georgiann Minster * George Conner * Greg Colucci * Hayley Rankin * Harold Garcia * Heidi Arnold * Irma Ranee Coy * Jacqueline Moss * Jan Kimball * Janice Schneider * Janice Spoor * Jennifer Redmond * Jessica Keown-Belous * Jim Beck * Jo Boguslaw * Jo Turner * Joanne Marie Turner * John Peiffer * John Wisbiski * Joseph Wauro * Joyce Stacy * Joyce Trifiletti * Judy Franklin * Judy Travers * Judy Padgett * Julie Heath * Junnahvee Benson * Karen Dahl * Karen Grams * Karen Higham * Karen Kaiser * Karen Meinburg Richwine * Karen Kirkman Parker * Karin Hawkins * Karin Vasvari * Kathleen Donohue Roesing * Kathleen Riddle-Wolfe * Kathy Hinds Moore * Kathy Jones * Kathy Mitchell * Katie Benzler * Kay Burns * Kelly Garcia * Ken Boggs * Keota Rodriguez * Kiera Mccarthy * Kim Estes * Kitty Stolle * Kristie Sciler * Kirsty Stanton * LaLonnie Scallen * Larry Morris * Leann Parr * Lenora Scales * Leslie Marie Jackson * Linda Forester * Linda Ingle Cox * Linda Kennerö * Linda Magill * Lisa Bower * Liz Gibson * Lorraine Wiman * Loretta Alexander * Lynda Bowles * Lynette Lawrance * LuAnn Louttit * Manny Rothman * Marcia Gibson DeWitt * Marie Calder * Marlene Bryan * MaryLouise Kramp * Mary Lynn Gross * Megan Atkins * Meghan Hyden * Melody Cannavan * Michael Carruthers * Michael Dinkens * Michael Vannoy * Michelle Burns-Mitchell * Michelle Pilcher * Micki Potter * Mike Moats * Mimi Baur * Myrna Hecht * Nadine Sutton * Nancy Ellen Sayre * Natalie Quine * Neena Martin * O'Della Wilson * Pat Pollington * Pat Rohn * Patricia Jarmon * Patricia C Trezza * Patrick Barry * Paul Lawrance * Peggy Davis * Phyllis Bassett * Raylene Matheny *

Talk Show Murders

Rebecca Collins Besner * Renee Brumley * Reta Hanna * Reta Moats * Roberta Navarro-Harder * Sally Berneathy * Sally Hubler * Sarah Santos * Satka Nikc * Sharon E. Edwards * Sharon Mangini * Sharon McMillon * Sheena Rawl * Sherry Amstutz * Shirley Alvarez * Shirley Davies * Shirley Williams * Stacie Rowe * Stephanie Conner * Steve Cullen * Susan Haughton * Susan Hesse Adams * Susan Salomon * Suzan K Chase * Taisha Cullum * Tamara Moore * Tammy Castleberry * Tammy Lynn Wood * Ted Murphy * Terri Atkins * Terri Creech * Terry Raab * Tonia Rachael Riggs-Williams * Travis Fleury-Lopez * Twyla Gawlas * Val Brooks * Walt Munsel * Yvonne Isakson *

Thank you to all these wonderful people.

Thank you for purchasing this book. I hope you enjoy it as much as I enjoyed writing it for my faithful readers. Please feel free to email me to tell me what you thought about my stories. I love hearing from the readers. I can be reached at murdernovels@bobmoats.com thanks again!